JESSICA'S CHRISTMAS KISS

When Jessica was fifteen, she shared a magical kiss with a mystery boy at a Christmas party. Now almost thirty, she is faced with a less than magical Christmas after uncovering her husband's secret affair. And, whilst she wouldn't admit it, she sometimes finds herself thinking about that perfect Christmas kiss, back when her life still seemed full of hope and possibility. But she never would have guessed that the boy she kissed in the kitchen all those years ago might still think about her too . . .

ALISON MAY

JESSICA'S CHRISTMAS KISS

Complete and Unabridged

LINFORD
Leicester

First published in Great Britain in 2016 by
Choc Lit Limited
Surrey

First Linford Edition
published 2018
by arrangement with
Choc Lit Limited
Surrey

*A catalogue record for this book is available
from the British Library.*

ISBN 978–1–4448–3939–5

Published by
F. A. Thorpe (Publishing)
Anstey, Leicestershire

Set by Words & Graphics Ltd.
Anstey, Leicestershire
Printed and bound in Great Britain by
T. J. International Ltd., Padstow, Cornwall

This book is printed on acid-free paper

For Paul

Acknowledgements

Immense thanks first of all to everyone at Choc Lit, especially to my lovely editor who has held my hand through all three *Christmas Kiss* novellas.

Thanks also to all those lovely people who make writing a less solitary experience — all my RNA, ADC and Pen Club friends, particularly Janet, Lisa and Holly who are always there with wine/cake/sympathy as required.

And finally, thanks, as always, to EngineerBoy for so very many different things.

A special thanks to the Tasting Panel readers who were the first to meet Holly, Cora and Jessica and made this all possible: Georgie, Michelle T., Leanne, Sarah A., Dorothy, Betty, Jennie H., Isabelle, Linda Sp., Christie, Jen, Olivia,

Sammi, Nicky, Rosie, Linda G., Hrund, Sally C. and Cindy.

Prologue

Christmas Eve, 2000

The perfect boy had dyed black hair that flopped in front of his face, not quite obscuring a pair of bright green eyes. He wore a single silver earring and black trousers and a faded T-shirt. He reminded her of the goths and indie kids at school. Jess sometimes wished she had the confidence to dress like them; standing out in a cool and uniform way was totally the best sort of fitting in.

He was leaning on the kitchen worktop next to the bottles of soft drink and pile of plastic cups. Jess poured her own drink. She could go back into the living room with the grown-ups and that Slade song playing on a constant loop. There was no reason to stay in the kitchen with a stranger. She made a deal in her head. If he spoke in the next five seconds then she'd stay. One . . . two . . . three . . . four . . . fi —

'So you know this Janine then?' He had the slightest hint of a local accent, hidden under something else. American maybe. It sounded amazing.

'She used to work with my dad. What about you?'

He shook his head. 'I came with a friend.'

'Right.' They fell into silence. Jess could run back to the party but somehow she didn't want to. She wanted to find out more about the boy in the kitchen. 'So what school do you go to?'

'Er . . . I went to Colesworth.'

'That's primary. What about now?'

He shook his head. 'I don't go to school any more.'

Jess's stomach flipped. He must be older than her then. An older boy. She sighed. 'Sixth form? University?'

'No. I'm working.'

He was so grown-up. Jess beamed.

2

'What do you do?'

He shrugged. 'Nothing exciting. What about you?'

Jess dropped her gaze to the floor. 'I'm still at school. Septon Grove.' He was going to think she was a stupid kid, wasn't he? 'I'm in my last year though.'

He sipped his coke. 'So what's school like?'

She shrugged. 'It's school. S'boring.' She glanced around the pine and laminate kitchen. 'My whole life's boring. It's just normal, you know.'

A smile spread across his face. 'It sounds great.'

'S'not.'

'I don't believe that. Tell me about your life.'

Jess scanned his face for the inevitable twitch of a laugh at the side of his lips, or the look in his eye that would give away the fact that he was mocking her. It wasn't there. He looked interested. People generally weren't very interested in Jess. She was dull. She knew that. She wasn't a high academic achiever like her oldest brother, or a great creative talent like the youngest. She was just Jess.

'Seriously. I'm interested.'

She squirmed. 'What in?'

'Christmas. Tell me about what you're doing for Christmas.'

So she did. She talked about her mum and dad and the well-rehearsed routines of Christmas Day. She talked about the sorts of presents she hoped for and the sorts of presents she might actually get. She told him about her trio of perfect brothers, and she admitted that sometimes being the baby and the only girl made her feel out of place and unsure of her role.

He nodded at that.

'You know what I mean?'

'Sometimes when there's a lot of people who want you to be a certain thing, it's hard to try to be anything else.'

'Exactly.' Jess paused. She'd never tried to put this into words before. 'It's not even that they want you to be that

4

thing. It's just that that's what they think you are.'

'Yeah. And then you end up becoming the thing they think you are. Even if you're not, but then you sort of are and . . . ' The beautiful black-haired boy's voice tailed away. 'I'm not really making sense any more, am I?'

'You are to me.'

'Cool.'

They were both still leaning on the worktop, but Jess realised that he was moving ever so slightly closer to her. She twisted to face him. His body was inches away from hers. He bent his head ever so slightly towards her. 'Is this okay?'

It took a second to realise what *this* was. This was it, wasn't it? It was actually happening. She'd come to a party and she'd met a boy. This was the beginning. Jess nodded. It was more than okay. She tilted her head and let him press his lips against hers. They were warm and firm, and they tasted of coca cola and salt and vinegar crisps, and it turned out that they were the absolute most perfect things for lips to taste of.

Jess leant further into the kiss, parting her lips ever so slightly, like she'd practised, so he could kiss her more deeply. She felt his hand move to her cheek and then to the back of her head. And then he pulled away.

'Sorry.' He was staring suddenly at the floor.

'No. Don't be. It was . . . ' Jess didn't have the words. 'Did I do it wrong?'

She saw the horror on his face. 'No. You were great. You are great. I . . . ' He glanced around the kitchen. 'Your parents are through there.'

'Right. Yeah.' He was right, of course. If Jess's mum or dad walked in on her kissing a boy she'd never met before at a party they'd probably keel over right there and then. 'Okay.'

He looked up and their eyes met for a second. He smiled. Jess's nerves calmed. 'I guess we should probably go back through then.'

He nodded. 'Sorry. You didn't say your name.'

She felt herself blushing. 'I'm Jess.'

He grinned. 'Hi Jess.'

'And yours?'

His brow furrowed instantly. 'What?'

'Your name?'

'Erm . . . '

'You've forgotten it.' She prodded him playfully on the arm and then pulled her hand away; the boy grabbed it, wrapping his fingers around her own.

'No. I know. It's . . . er . . . ' He hesitated again. 'Alan. I'm Alan.'

★   ★   ★

He kept hold of her hand as long as he could, until finally the distance was too great and he had no choice but to release her. She flashed a smile back over her shoulder. She thought he was going to be there in a second. She thought that before they went home they'd probably exchange numbers, and that after Christmas he'd ring and

7

they'd go and hang out at McDonalds or the shopping centre or whatever it was that normal teenagers did. Was it kinder to let her think that? Lucas wasn't sure.

He was sure that he couldn't follow her back into the living room. If he did then every second in that room was a second more risk of somebody recognising him, or of the mate he'd got dragged along with getting careless and calling him Lucas, and when people knew who he was everything changed. Everything always changed. Lucas knew what he had to do. He had to walk out of the back door, call a cab and get himself back to the hotel, and then he had to forget about the blonde girl with the perfect coca-cola lips.

Lucas paused at the back door, his unfamiliar reflection with its newly dyed hair staring back at him. It was one kiss. It didn't mean anything. As soon as the thought came he wished it away. He shouldn't be this cynical this young, but he'd been kissed a lot. Not by girls his own age, not with warmth or affection or desire. He'd been kissed by producers, and agents, and money-men, and co-stars, and by endless people who were always around and who apparently had some reason for being where Lucas was and for bending and planting air kisses in the vicinity of his cheeks. Kissing him like a gambler might kiss the dice for luck, hoping to absorb a little bit of whatever it was that had made Lucas, fleetingly, the most famous kid on the planet. Cheek-kiss after cheek-kiss from a parade of strangers who told him they were friends.

Lucas opened the back door. It might be cynical. He might not like it, but he knew it was right. Kisses didn't mean anything.

Lucas made his way around the side of the house and into the street. It was cold, and ice was forming on the puddles in the gutter. He glanced at his watch. 11.45 p.m. Nearly Christmas Day. He wondered what the normal people were doing. Probably spending their evening at parties, rather than running away from one. His mobile phone buzzed in his pocket. What now? Probably his mate trying to find out where he'd disappeared to. He answered the call without looking properly at the screen. 'I'm sorry. I needed . . . '

A stranger's voice interrupted him. 'Is this Lucas Woods?'

'Er . . . yeah.'

The voice at the other end of the line giggled for a second. 'Sorry. Mr Woods, I'm calling from the Monarch car service.'

Lucas frowned. He'd got in the habit of using the car service when he came back to the UK, back when the studio were picking up the bill. He hadn't used them for months though. 'Right?'

'I'm afraid there's been an incident with a vehicle on your account.'

Lucas shook his head. 'No. I haven't booked a car.'

The woman was insistent. 'One of our drivers was booked to collect you from . . . hold on one sec . . . from the

Central Leeds Plaza at 8 p.m.?'

That didn't make any sense. 'No. I've been out with a friend all evening.'

'I'm sorry sir. The booking was on your account.'

Lucas realised what that meant. His account wasn't him, was it? He closed his eyes for a second before answering. 'You said there was an incident.'

'Yes.' The woman hesitated. 'I'm afraid the vehicle appears to have been stolen.'

Lucas was confused again. You booked a car from Monarch with a driver. The car belonged to them. Why was it his problem if one got stolen? 'What do you mean?'

'I mean that the gentleman who booked the vehicle appears to have taken it.'

All Lucas wanted was to head back into the party and be a normal sixteen year old. He wanted to be back in that kitchen listening to a beautiful girl moaning about how lame her parents were. He wanted to be eating crisps and

11

trying to flick peanuts straight into his mouth. He wanted to be anxious about exams and whether to go to university. He wanted to be that boy in the kitchen that nobody knew. He wanted to be Alan. He didn't want to be Lucas Woods.

The woman on the other end of the line was still talking. 'I have to ask Mr Woods. Do you know who the gentleman might be?'

Lucas tried to swallow down the anxiety that was rising from his belly. 'It might be my dad,' he said.

2014

1

23rd December, 2014

Lucas

'How is he today?'

The nurse shrugged. 'He's fine. A bit cranky still, since we put the decorations up. He still won't have any in his room.'

Lucas nodded. It was the same every year. The Christmas trees and tinsel sparked half-formed memories of better days and worse. You never quite knew how he was going to react.

The nurse smiled encouragingly. 'He's in his room.'

Right. There wasn't really any reason to hesitate. Lucas had been visiting this place every day since he'd moved himself and his dad to London five years earlier. Leeds had been fine, but he'd been too conspicuous. It was too easy to be recognised. The capital was better, and he'd been twenty-five by the time he'd moved down here. Nearly a decade had passed since his last film. Fifteen years since the one that had made him a temporary star. His face had filled out and he'd taken to maintaining a shadow of stubble across his jaw. He answered to his adopted name as naturally as to his real one. He barely even recognised Lucas Woods when he looked in the mirror any more.

Lucas knocked lightly on the door of room twelve before pushing it open. 'Hello?'

His dad was sitting in the good chair at the far side of the lounge area. The nurses and careworkers called them 'rooms', but really the residents here had suites comparable with most good hotels. There was a bedroom, a sitting room and a bathroom. Some of the apartments even had a kitchen. This one didn't. After the fire at the last place Lucas had decided that wasn't a good idea. His dad looked up as he came in. 'I thought you'd forgotten about me.'

Lucas forced himself to smile. So guilt was going to be the mood for the visit. 'Of course not. I was here yesterday. Remember?'

His father didn't respond. Lucas sat opposite him. 'So did you have a good night?'

A shrug.

'Okay. I was working on the helpline yesterday.' Lucas listened to himself trying to make some sort of conversation. 'It was pretty quiet. I'm at the advice centre this afternoon.'

'Bloody do-gooder.'

'I like to keep busy.'

Lucas watched his dad stare out of the window. He wasn't an old man at all. Forty-five. Only fifteen years older than the son he was so keen to ignore. Lucas realised that he, himself, was nearly the same age now as his dad was when he'd had the crash. He was embarking on the life that his father had missed out on. 'I got a Christmas card from the twins.'

His father didn't reply. Lucas couldn't even be sure that he remembered who his son was talking about. Some days the memories seemed as fresh and raw to his dad as they remained to Lucas. Some days he either didn't know, or didn't care. 'Ruth's getting married again, apparently. You remember her? The mum.'

Again he got no response. Lucas could still picture Ruth's face, wracked with grief even as her voice was telling him it wasn't his fault. She'd been kind, but she'd been wrong. All of this was Lucas's fault. He'd done everything he could to make it right, but there were some debts that even the kid whose wildest dreams came true couldn't repay.

'They won't let me go out.'

Lucas closed his eyes. 'You can go out if you want. I'll come and take you out.'

His dad shook his head. 'I don't need you to take me.'

'Well Carys then.' Carys was his dad's favourite carer. 'I can pay her extra to take you out on her day off. We've done that before.'

'She's gone.'

Lucas frowned. He was sure he'd seen Carys in the hallway on his way to his dad's room. 'I don't think she has.'

His father had gone back to staring sullenly out of the window. 'Well she won't come and talk to me. I get this big bloke now.'

'Well I'm sure there's a good reason.' Worryingly, Lucas really was sure there was a good reason. He spent a few more fruitless minutes trying to talk to his father, before heading out. Carys was leaning on the desk in the main lobby shuffling through some papers. Lucas hesitated. He didn't know her that well. She was very young, but seemed to cope better with the work than a lot of the young girls who arrived and disappeared again after two weeks when they discovered the realities of the job. 'Excuse me.'

She turned. 'Oh. Hi.'

'I wanted to check something. My dad says you're not caring for him anymore.'

Her gaze fixed itself somewhere to the left of Lucas's shoulder. 'No. I thought Julia was going to talk to you about that.'

Julia was the manager. Lucas shook his head.

'Right. She's off today. Maybe you should talk to her after Christmas.'

Lucas's stomach tightened. His father had been moved from home to home over the last fifteen years. He was too disruptive, or his condition was too complex, or his behaviour was too much for the staff. Lucas wasn't sure his dad would cope with another move. 'Just tell me what the problem is?'

He caught the hint of frustration in his voice, and forced himself to take a deep breath. 'I mean, I'm sure whatever it was wasn't your fault.'

The girl's cheeks flushed pink. 'No. It wasn't.'

18

'Right. But what happened?'

'Mr Woods . . . well, you know he got hold of some whisky last month.'

Lucas nodded. It wasn't the staff's fault. His dad was an addict. He was an addict with the brain of a child trapped inside an adult's body. If he could find drink, he would. 'Well, it wasn't so much the drinking that was the problem. He tried to . . . '

Lucas desperately wanted to block his ears. He couldn't. ' . . . he tried to touch me on the . . . ' Her voice tailed off. 'You know. He was quite . . . ' She hesitated again. 'I was scared.'

'I'm really sorry.'

She nodded. 'It's not your fault. Anyway it's fine. I shoved him away, and pressed the buzzer. Julia and one of the blokes from estates were there before anything really happened.'

'Good. Right. I'm sorry though.'

The girl shrugged. 'Julia was supposed to talk to you. Explain why we'd changed around.'

'That's fine. I know now. I'm so sorry.'

'No need.' She picked up her bundle of papers. 'I'd better get on.'

'Right. Of course.'

'Merry Christmas.'

He nodded. 'Same to you.'

He walked out into the chilly air feeling grim. Maybe, whatever he told himself, this wasn't for the best. Maybe it was time to admit that and find a house where he could care for his dad himself. He thought back to when he'd tried before, rubbing his fingers over the bridge of his nose where he could still feel the bump from the years old broken bone. He was older now though, if not wiser. Maybe things would be different.

23rd December, 2014

Jessica

Christmas drinks before Michelle and Sean headed up to Scotland. Jess took a deep breath. It was nice, just her and her best friend, her best friend's husband,

and the youngest of Jess's three big brothers, Simon. These were probably the three people she was closest to in the world. Apart from her husband, of course.

Simon picked up a card from the pile on the table between them. 'Okay. The question is . . . your first kiss? Truth or dare?'

Jess shook her head and sipped her wine. 'I don't think so.'

Her best friend, Michelle, and Michelle's husband, Sean, stared at her expectantly. 'Why not?'

'Because you're sober, so I'm at a disadvantage. And you already know anyway.'

Michelle patted her growing belly. 'Well I'm only sober because of this little one. And Sean doesn't know.'

Simon laughed. 'And I'm not sober, so it all works out.'

Jess shook her head. 'I thought it was Sean's turn anyway.'

There was a second of silence, before Jess realised why Sean wasn't talking. Sean's first kiss would have been with his childhood sweetheart, wouldn't it?

An image popped, uninvited, into Jess's head. *Cora.* She tightened her grip on her wine glass. 'What about you Simon?'

'It's not my turn.'

Jess pursed her lips. 'Well I'll tell mine, if you tell yours.'

Her brother shook his head. 'Well there were a couple of girls during school, but my first proper kiss was a boy called Craig on the school residential trip to Norfolk.' He grinned. 'I saw him again a couple of years after when I was with Anthony, who was insanely jealous of course.'

The group fell quiet for a second. Anthony had been Simon's first, and only, serious boyfriend. He'd died, after a long illness, when Jess was in her teens, but she could still picture her brother's devastation.

Simon broke the silence. 'Right. Your turn.'

Jess took a drink. 'Fine.' She closed her eyes for a second and thought back. 'It was 2000 I think. It was Christmas

Eve, so I was fifteen.'

'Quite old.'

'Fifteen's not that old.'

'It is,' Sean insisted.

'Well maybe if you grow up with nothing but trees for miles around and there's nothing else to do.'

He opened his mouth to protest before Michelle whacked him over the head with a cushion. 'Let her tell her story.'

'Thank you. Anyway I was fifteen. It was Christmas Eve. I was at some horrible party at this friend of my mum's house.' She turned towards her brother. 'Aunty Janine, you know?'

Simon shook his head. 'Not a clue. Definitely not a proper aunty.'

Jess pursed her lips. The twelve year age gap between her and her youngest brother meant that more often than not their childhood memories failed to overlap. 'Well anyway, it was all vol-au-vents and mini sausage rolls . . . '

'I like a mini sausage roll.'

Jess shrugged. 'Well everyone likes a

mini sausage roll. That's not the point. Anyway it was a horrible party, and I was in a massive sulk because I hadn't been allowed to go to Keeley Andrew's party at her house which everyone in our year went to.'

Michelle pursed her lips. 'I didn't.'

Jess grinned. 'That's because you refused to engage in any form of Christmas celebration. All the normal people in our year went.'

'Get to the point.'

'Sorry. So anyway, it was in the kitchen. He had dyed hair and an earring, so I basically thought he was the most worldly and glamorous being I'd ever met.'

'So you snogged him?'

Jess didn't meet Sean's eye. 'I did. And so that's that. My first kiss story.'

But of course that wasn't quite that, was it? Jess let her mind take her back to that kitchen, and that boy with the shock of black hair hanging in front of his bright green eyes. She remembered the touch of his fingers against her cheek, and the taste of his lips — cheap cola and a hint of salt. She remembered the cheesy Christmas music coming through the wall. She remembered the cupboard door handle that had been digging into her side, and she remembered not caring at all. She remembered friends at school describing their first kisses as gross or sloppy or icky, but hers had been nothing like that. It had been warm and soft and she'd felt somehow like she'd arrived home. She wondered if she'd ever been kissed like that since.

'What was his name?' Sean interrupted her thoughts.

Jess heard Michelle and Simon snigger. 'She doesn't know.'

'What?' Sean frowned.

'I do know. He was called Alan.'

Michelle shook her head. 'Only you checked and there was nobody called Alan at that party.'

Sean grinned. 'You got fake named.'

'I did not.'

Michelle was staring down at her glass, but Jess could see the smirk pulling at her best friend's lips.

'Well I never met him again anyway. He was there at that party and then he was gone.'

'Oh I get it.' Sean was grinning. 'He's the one that got away.'

Simon nodded vigorously. 'That's what I said.'

'Wise man. One perfect kiss and then he vanishes. Definitely the one that got away.'

Michelle sighed. 'You are such a girl when it comes to romance.'

'And you have no soul.'

Jess let them replay their regular argument. Of course the boy at the party wasn't her 'one that got away'. Okay, so she might have thought that once, but she wasn't a teenager any more. She was an adult and that meant not getting swept away by silly romantic ideas. There was no perfect guy out there pining for her. There was her husband, Patrick, and she was going to find ways to compromise, and they were going to make things work. That was realistic, not some hopeless teenage fantasy. Another memory forced itself to the front of Jess's mind. Cora. Was she Patrick's 'one that got away'?

Jess had actually been to confront the other woman, and had instantly regretted it. Cora's apartment was a penthouse on the South Bank, and the woman herself was a picture of old school glamour. Perfect chestnut-brown hair, creamy skin, and the sort of figure that would have made Cindy Crawford look a bit frumpy. Jess was a scruffy, dowdy mess by comparison. And rather than Cora apologising to Jess for trying to steal her husband, Jess had found herself apologising for taking him back. Nothing about the visit had worked out like she'd imagined it.

Michelle glanced at the clock. 'I guess we'd better get going.'

A knot formed in Jess's stomach. Her friends wanted to leave before Patrick got back. He'd gone for a drink with some friends from where he used to work, at least that's what he'd told her.

Jess took a deep breath. That's what he'd told her, and she believed him, like she believed him every time he popped out to see a recruitment agent, or go for a run, or to the gym. On the settee, Sean glanced at his watch and raised an eyebrow to his wife. Even he didn't want to stay, and he was Patrick's best mate. At least he had been. Was it always going to be like this? Jess frowned. 'You could stay to say hello.'

The look they exchanged was fleeting but Jess saw it. Michelle shook her head. 'It's not that. We've got a long drive tomorrow. Back to Scotland for Christmas.'

A noise in the hallway interrupted Jess's reply. 'That must be him now.'

She pulled herself to her feet and dashed the four paces to the door. Patrick was peeling off layers of coat, scarf and gloves. He was handsome. Properly handsome. Underwear model handsome. She watched him run his fingers through his hair and waited for the pang of desire she was used to feeling to hit her. It didn't quite come. Jess pushed the corners of her mouth wide. 'Michelle and Sean are still here. And Simon.'

Patrick nodded and flashed his perfectly even smile. 'Great.'

Jess followed her husband into the lounge. He asked after Sean's business and Michelle's health. Both replied grudgingly. Jess could feel her muscles tightening. Patrick was trying to put everything with . . . her brain pushed the details of the thought away . . . Patrick was trying to put everything that had happened behind them. She could see that he was trying. Why wouldn't her friends see that too?

She took a deep breath. The fairy lights were twinkling on the Christmas tree in the corner. Her present for Patrick was wrapped and waiting. In a couple of days it would be Christmas and then New Year. Once January came they really would be able to make a fresh start. All she had to do was hold on until then.

2

Christmas Eve, 2014

Lucas

'Alan!' Lucas didn't hesitate before responding to the name.

'What's up?'

His supervisor, Viv, held a green form out towards him. 'You couldn't see one more, could you?'

Lucas sighed. It was nearly lunchtime. The morning hadn't been busy. Christmas Eve morning never was, but the people who did come in were in genuine crisis. 'I'm supposed to be going to see my dad.'

Viv pulled a face. 'I know. But there's only you and Gwen still here, and she's got two cases to write up.' Lucas looked across the office at his colleague. Gwen was lovely, fantastic with the clients — she'd taught Lucas a lot when he first started, but she was notoriously slow on the computer. She'd probably still be writing up her notes on Christmas morning. Viv held out the form. 'And I'd really really like to get home at some point this afternoon.'

Lucas nodded.

'Thanks.' Viv grinned. 'I can always rely on you.'

He picked up the form and scanned the details. A new client. Housing issue. No other details. Great. He headed into the waiting room. There was only one person waiting. Lucas had long ago stopped trying to guess clients' ages. Life put lines on people's faces that time couldn't justify. Lucas led the man into an interview room and gestured for him to take a seat. As he waited a stench of sweat and stale alcohol settled around the room. Lucas swallowed. 'So you've got a housing problem you're wanting some help with?'

The man nodded. 'Not got anywhere to stay.'

'You're homeless?'

'That's what I said.'

Lucas ran through his questions, to increasingly brief and irritated answers, and established that the man had been released from prison, and had been promised that his probation officer would find him temporary accommodation. He established that the man had a brother who lived locally, but couldn't stay there because the terms of his probation forbade him from contacting family members. Lucas didn't question why and he kept his expression as neutral as possible. He was here to help, not to judge. 'Okay. If you can hold on there for a few minutes, I'll see what options we can find you.'

Lucas left the man in the interview room and went back into the office. It was after lunchtime on Christmas Eve. His chances of getting anything from the council were slim to non-existent. A call to the probation service confirmed that the client's probation officer was off work and there was no temporary accommodation available that anyone else could arrange. It was going to be a question of night shelters and rough sleepers' charities. Lucas made a few more calls, grabbed a map and then went back to his client. 'There's spaces at the night shelter here.' He marked the location on the map. 'And they're doing Christmas dinner tomorrow in the community centre next door. Do you think that would be all right?'

The man shrugged.

'And can you get there okay?'

'Dunno. How far is it?'

Lucas drew another circle on the map to show where they were now. 'It's not that far. Are you all right walking?'

'Walking's all I can do.' The man peered at the map. 'Got chucked out of my last hostel for the booze.'

Lucas nodded. 'Do you want any help with that?'

'Had help before. It doesn't last.'

Lucas watched the man shuffle out into the cold. He hadn't done much. Every day he hoped that today might be the day he made everything better for someone, and every day he made a suggestion here and a compromise there. It was always one night out of the cold and a hot meal tomorrow, but never anything more.

The man stopped outside and turned back. 'Well Happy Christmas mate.'

'Happy Christmas.' Lucas closed the centre door behind the client, dropped the latch and pushed the two bolts across. So the guy had had help for his drinking before. What had he said? *It doesn't last.*

That wasn't true. Lucas had seen people who'd got off drink, or drugs, and stayed sober for decades. There were volunteers he'd worked with who were alcoholics themselves but were managing to leave their addiction behind. It had to be achievable. He just needed to find the right support, the right programme, the right help. He glanced at the clock. If he wrote his notes up quickly he still had time to see his dad. Maybe he'd be in a better mood today.

Christmas Eve, 2014

Jessica

Jess was ready too early. Of course she was ready too early. She'd been up at six o'clock, at the supermarket by six-thirty, and back home, cleaning the oven, soon after seven. She'd noted the hint of laughter in Patrick's expression when she'd made him lift his feet up so she could vacuum in front of the settee, and she'd ignored it. It wasn't *his* mother who was about to descend on the flat. Jess reconsidered the thought. *At least* it wasn't his mother who was about to descend on the flat.

And Patrick had helped. He'd put the beers and wine she'd bought in the fridge. Okay, so he'd helped himself to one while he was there, but it was, as he'd pointed out, Christmas Eve. You were allowed a sneaky beer on Christmas Eve. And now he'd gone to get some flowers to, in his words, brighten the place up. To be fair, Patrick had always been generous. Their relationship had been on and off for years before they'd finally got engaged, and every time they got together again he would woo her with gifts and flowers. Jess was aware that plenty of her friends — wise only after the event — were now convinced that Patrick's lack of early commitment was a warning sign. She was equally aware that they were wrong. It hadn't been Patrick dragging his feet for all those years.

Jess surveyed the tiny living room, trying to picture it from her mother's point of view. It was a disappointment. She knew that, but a single wage didn't get you very far in London. The fact that they had a second bedroom that they'd somehow managed to crowbar a double bed into was a hangover from the days when Patrick was working full time as well. When they'd looked at the flat Jess had thought it would make a nice nursery. A lot had happened since then.

She busied herself plumping up cushions and straightening the Christmas cards blu-tacked to the back of the door. As she lifted the cushion at the far end of the sofa, something caught her eye. Half-wedged down the side of the seat was a sleek black rectangle. She picked it up and placed it carefully on the arm of the settee. Patrick's phone.

Jess sat down in the armchair at the other side of the room and tried not to stare at the handset. It reminded her of the diet she'd been on before the wedding. She was fine, so long as there were no cakes or biscuits in the house, but as soon as there were, they would call to her. The idea that she could have half a piece would burrow into her head and refuse to go away, and then half a piece would become a whole piece, and, more often than not, two or three pieces. The phone was like that. It was goading her to take a look. It was tempting her to quickly check his texts. It would be so easy. She could sneak a peek at his call list and his contacts. Just to put her mind at rest. She jumped out of her chair and grabbed the phone. They didn't have secrets any more, did they? That's what he'd promised. So it wasn't snooping if he didn't have anything to hide. Her finger hovered over the unlock key. Only, if there weren't any secrets, what was she expecting to find?

The sound of Patrick's key in the lock made her jump. She dropped the phone onto the sofa and pulled the cushion over it. 'I'm back. And look who I found outside.'

Her parents followed Patrick into the living room, an already weary-looking Simon trailing behind. Patrick smiled broadly, full of festive spirit. 'I'll get some drinks.'

Jess's mum cast an obviously appraising gaze around the room. 'Very nice dear. You've decorated since we were last here.'

It was true. She'd painted most of the flat by herself one weekend in October. She'd wanted to make everything clean and fresh and new. She nodded brightly and told herself it was working.

Patrick re-appeared from the kitchen.

She'd thought he was making tea, but the tray in front of him had a bottle of bubbly and five champagne flutes. He popped the cork to appreciative murmurs. 'I know it's a couple of days since our anniversary, but I thought a little pre-Christmas, post-wedding anniversary celebration was in order.'

Jess let him pour her a glass. They'd got married on the 22nd December. A year and two days ago. That was all. They were still newlyweds really. He'd bought her a necklace for their anniversary. She fingered the pendant at her neck. Jewellery, champagne and Patrick was all smiles. Maybe she'd been right when she'd told . . . her mind pushed the name away . . . when she'd told that woman that it was a blip. Maybe Patrick had just been struggling to adapt to married life. She'd decided to make this work. Now she needed to work on believing that he was doing the same.

She let the pendant drop against her collar bone. He'd told her the necklace was silver, but the label he'd left in the bag said platinum, and they were drinking proper champagne not Prosecco or Asti. She didn't know where the money had come from. She had to stop thinking like that. She never used to be a suspicious person. She'd simply loved Patrick and she'd known that he loved her. He'd probably have married her while they were still at university, but Jess had said they were too young. You had to be sensible about love when you were starting out. Jess had seen friends make all the mistakes in the book. She'd seen people rush in to relationships; she'd seen people diving into something on the rebound; she'd even seen people tear themselves apart trying to make long-distance work. Jess hadn't done any of those things. She'd waited until they both had jobs in London. She'd waited until they could afford to buy a flat, and when she'd accepted his proposal she'd thought that that was that. She didn't think she needed to worry that he wasn't where he said he was, or wonder whether the little gifts he brought her were inspired by guilt rather than affection. Now she wondered about everything.

Her husband moved to stand beside her and clinked his glass against hers. 'Happy Christmas.'

She smiled, and opened her mouth to return the good wishes. Patrick frowned, and patted his jeans' pocket. 'Have you seen my phone?'

Jess took a sip of champagne and shook her head.

3

Christmas Eve, 2014

Lucas

'We've been waiting for you.' Two of Lucas's three flatmates were already huddled up on the settee when he got in.

He glanced at the clock. 'Sorry. I was . . . ' He didn't tend to tell his flatmates that much about his life. They were good friends but there was stuff he preferred not to share. His background. His work history. His real name. They knew, he presumed, that he had a dad, and they knew he did voluntary work, and they speculated wildly about how he managed to make the rent without any obvious source of income, but they were generally refreshingly happy to let him be. 'I had a couple of things to sort out.'

Trish, the de facto mum of the household, shook her dreadlock covered head. 'You're disrespecting Christmas film night.'

Lucas grinned. 'It's about the eighth Christmas film night we've had this month.'

Trish's girlfriend, Charlie, rolled her eyes. 'And your point is?'

In truth, he had no point to make. He'd learned from experience that only a fool got between Charlie and a festive movie. He grabbed a beer from the fridge and settled on the sofa. He spent a good amount of his childhood in trailers and hotel rooms, never quite knowing where his roots were. Their shared house was on the shabby side, but it was closer to being home than anywhere else he'd lived in the last two decades. He took a swig of beer. A quiet Christmas with undemanding people who wouldn't ask too many questions . . .

'Anyway, before the film, Charlie has a new theory!' Trish prodded him in the ribs.

'Really?'

Charlie grinned. 'I think you escaped from Alcatraz.'

'What?'

'There were these three guys who escaped from Alcatraz in the sixties, and were like never seen again.'

'The sixties?'

She nodded.

'So you think I escaped from a high security prison on an island off San Francisco fifty years ago.'

'It's the only logical explanation, Fake Alan.'

The 'Fake' had been added to his name a few days after he'd moved in. Charlie had been standing in the hallway yelling his name repeatedly, before she marched into his room and demanded to know why he wasn't replying. He'd hesitated, only for a second, but it was long enough. Her eyes had narrowed. 'It's not your real name, is it?'

'What?' Lucas had been astonished. Nobody had ever called him out on the lie before. 'Course it is.'

Charlie had laughed. 'Bollocks.'

And so, somehow, he'd become Fake Alan, first at home and then at the pub on the corner, and the shop opposite, and then with Mrs Kingsley next door. And yet the story of who he really was, and why he called himself Alan had never been told. Sometimes, when all the beers had been drunk and they were toying with opening one of the random liqueurs from the back of the cupboard, Trish or Charlie would offer a theory. He was in witness protection. He was undercover. He was an alien sent to investigate earth culture. And Lucas would laugh and the conversation would move on. The Alcatraz theory was a new variation of the oft-repeated idea that he was, for some reason, on the run. 'You know that I'd have to be about eighty for that to make sense.'

Charlie tapped her nose. 'Plastic surgery. After your escape.'

Lucas shook his head. 'Just start the movie.'

'Cora's not here yet.'

Cora was the newest addition to the household. He'd helped her move her stuff in from some swanky place on the South Bank. Charlie had been very excited that they might have a wealthy flatmate, until Trish had pointed out that if Cora was rolling in money she wouldn't be renting a room off them. Lucas had kept his mouth shut.

Trish took a swig from her beer. 'She'll be mooning over Santa Claus.'

Cora had got herself a seasonal job at the department store Trish worked for, playing the part of Rudolph and was, quite clearly, smitten with the guy playing Father Christmas. Lucas nodded. 'She's right. We can't wait all night.'

'Fine.' Charlie stood up and pulled two DVDs from behind the telly. 'So we have Christmas classic, *Die Hard*, or we have *The Santa Clause 2*.'

Lucas shook his head. '*Die Hard* is not a Christmas film. It's a film that happens at Christmas. Not the same.'

Trish grabbed the other DVD. 'Well I

haven't seen *The Santa Clause 1*. I might not understand the second one.'

Charlie flicked the TV on, and scrolled through the programme guide. 'What about this? *Miracle at the North Pole* is on at half past.'

'That's a classic.' Trish nodded her approval. 'A proper Christmas movie.'

Her girlfriend shrugged. 'But everyone must have seen it like a million times.'

Lucas never had.

'I wonder what happened to the kid.'

'The actor?' Trish screwed up her nose. 'Didn't he have some kind of meltdown?'

Lucas let the conversation wash over him. *Miracle at the North Pole?* He'd managed to get to thirty without seeing it. It was one of those films that was on somewhere every Christmas. An instant classic apparently, but Lucas didn't believe in Christmas miracles. He grabbed a DVD box from Charlie's lap. 'You're right. Everyone's seen that. Let's do *Die Hard*.'

'You said *Die Hard* wasn't a Christmas film.'

He flipped open the case and slid the disc into the player. 'Then this is your chance to prove me wrong.'

Christmas Day, 2014

Jessica

Jess stirred her gravy. Last year it had been just her and Patrick and she'd given up part way through the process, and used granules out of a jar. This year her parents were here, and everything had to be right. On cue her mother appeared in the kitchen doorway. 'Are you sure you don't need any help dear?'

Jess shook her head. 'I'm fine.'

'Only we normally eat around one. Otherwise you're not done in time for the Queen.'

Jess glanced at the clock. 1.45 p.m. She could say that it didn't matter. She could point out that Christmas was about spending time together and it was fine to be relaxed about what time they ate. She made her lips into a smile. 'Nearly ready. Just letting the turkey rest.'

Jess wasn't a big cook, but she knew the turkey had to rest. When she'd first read that she'd thought it was a typo. The turkey was dead, but no, it turned out resting meat was a thing. It stopped it being tough and dry apparently, like cooking vegetables for less than three hours meant they tasted of something. Moving out of her mother's home had been a culinary revelation.

Simon appeared in the doorway. 'Come on. Let Jess get on with things.'

She mouthed a silent 'thank you' to her brother as he led their mum back into the living room, and turned her attention back to the gravy. It was nearly there. She pulled her list from where it was jammed under the corner of a dirty pan and smoothed it flat on the workshop. Starters were ready. Red wine was open on the table. White wine was in the fridge. The roasted veg needed another ten minutes. The turkey was done. Jess took a breath, untied her apron and picked up the tray of starter plates. 'Lunch is served.'

Her mum, dad and brother hauled themselves off the sofa and gathered around the dining table squashed into one corner of the lounge. Jess frowned. 'Where's Patrick?'

Simon shrugged. 'His phone rang. Think he went to answer it.'

The knot in Jess's stomach, that tightened every time her husband's phone rang unexpectedly, constricted even further. She handed the tray to her brother and plastered a smile on her lips. 'I'll go find him.'

In a flat the size of theirs finding Patrick wasn't difficult. Jess could hear his voice from the hallway, and followed the sound into the bedroom. He was on the balcony — well they called it the balcony; it was supposed to be a fire escape but the ladder was broken. She opened her mouth to call to him, and then closed it again. The knot hadn't loosened. Somebody had phoned her husband on Christmas Day. The only people who phoned on Christmas Day were parents and lovers, and he wouldn't be freezing himself half to death on the balcony to exchange seasonal good wishes with his mum.

Jess sat on the corner of the bed, feet away from the half-open door, and listened, waiting to be proven wrong. Patrick had promised after all. They'd made a fresh start, but the image she always carried with her swam in front of her eyes. Cora, Patrick's other woman. She corrected herself instantly. His former other woman. It was over. They were trying again. As always, the Cora in Jess's mind's eye was almost impossibly beautiful — Jess's polar opposite. Jess was short and, at best, curvy, or at worst, slightly plump. Her hair spun out in erratic blonde curls. Cora was tall with sleek brunette waves. Jess glanced down at her own body. She had a gravy stain on her nice top that she'd worn especially for Christmas lunch. How could she compete?

Through the door she could hear her husband mming and aahing. Clearly the other person was dominating the conversation. A shoot of hope jumped into her heart — maybe it was his mother after all. There were other things she could do. She could go back into the hallway and call to him that lunch was ready and then take her seat at the table with the others. She could choose not to know. That was what she'd promised. He'd promised that it was a one-off, and she'd promised to trust that. She'd promised not to snoop and pry. She'd even agreed that was for her benefit. Patrick had nothing to hide, so she'd only be torturing herself. All she needed to do was stand up and walk away.

Jess stayed sitting on the bed. She'd heard of the thing that happened in America. They called it suicide by cop. It was when someone was desperate to end it all, but couldn't quite bring themselves to pull the trigger, so they simply stepped outside, waved the gun in the direction of the police and waited for the inevitable. That was sort of what Jess was doing now. Checking his phone, following him, going through his credit card statement — those would have been like she was pulling the trigger herself. Sitting here, quietly listening, that was just accepting her inevitable fate.

'You know I can't.'

Jess's whole body stiffened at the sound of her husband's voice.

'You know why not . . . Because it's Christmas . . . Of course I'd rather be with you.'

A wave of nausea swept through Jess's body. This was it. All she had to do was let the truth wash over her.

'Seriously, her whole family are here. They're even more boring than her.'

Another wave of nausea. The moment to walk away had passed. Jess closed her eyes.

'Anyway, I'm gonna tell her. You know that. After Christmas it'll be you and me. A fresh start.'

A fresh start? Jess's mind seemed to float somewhere outside of her body, wafting around the bedroom on its own little cloud of serenity. Patrick had promised her a fresh start. Now he was promising it to someone else. It showed a sort of consistency, if you thought about it.

'Look, I gotta go. I love you babe.'

Jess opened her eyes as Patrick came back into the room. He stopped in the doorway, and she watched the split second it took his face to arrange itself into an utterly relaxed smile. 'What are you doing in here? I thought you'd be through there.' He flicked his eyes towards the kitchen. 'Dealing with lunch.'

Jess shook her head. 'Lunch is all ready.'

'Right then.' He walked past her towards the hallway. 'Are you coming then?'

'I'll be there in a minute.'

Patrick frowned. 'You weren't listening to me on the phone were you? We agreed. We have to trust each other.'

Jess thought for a second. 'I wasn't listening.' That was true. She hadn't set out to come in here and listen to him. She just happened to have heard. That was quite different.

'Good. It was my mum. She says Happy Christmas.'

'Okay.' Jess pointed at the stain on her top. 'I'm going to change this, and then I'll be through. You go and make a start.'

He nodded and she listened to his footsteps followed by the sounds of voices rising in the lounge. The lunch was done, and Simon was an excellent cook. She was sure he'd be able to find the brandy butter for the pudding and dish up the vegetables. Really everything was in hand. There was no reason for her to be here at all. Jess pulled a fleecy jumper off the back of the chair at her side of the bed and put it on. The little mini-satchel handbag she always carried outside of term-time was dumped on the same chair. She slung it across her body and stood up. There was really no need to make a fuss. There was definitely no need to spoil everyone else's Christmas. It was probably for the best for everyone if she slipped away.

She lifted the latch on the front door as quietly she could and then changed her mind. She quickly tiptoed back to the kitchen and pulled a bottle of Baileys from the cupboard. Then she stepped out into the stairwell. She'd always found Christmas dinner a bit much if she was honest. She didn't like the bloated feeling afterwards. A nice long walk would be far better for her, and the Baileys was very Christmassy so nobody could accuse her of not getting into the festive spirit. She unscrewed the cap and took a good long swig.

4

Christmas Day, 2014

Lucas

Lucas watched his dad pull the wrapping off his final present. It was a comic book. It was always a comic book. Years ago, before everything had changed, comic books had been one of their great shared loves. They could spend hours looking at comics and movie memorabilia. Lucas remembered being allowed to choose one comic book, with a strict price limit, and he remembered how his dad would pause over the special editions and rare copies that could run to hundreds of pounds. Maybe in another life his dad would have been a proper collector, but in this life he'd had a son, and until everything in both their lives had changed forever, every penny his dad had struggled to earn had been spent on Lucas.

Some years the comics were greeted with childlike glee and Lucas would get to share a few happy minutes poring over the artwork and the story. This year his dad threw the gift directly at Lucas, missing his ear by an inch at most. Lucas sighed. 'Well I'll put this on the table then. Maybe you'll want to look at it later.'

'Why do you come?'

'To see you Dad.'

'I don't want you here.' He glared at Lucas and then twisted his head away. 'All of this is your fault.'

Lucas swallowed. 'I know. I'm sorry.'

His dad turned back towards his son and spat a long stream of saliva in his direction. His face was turning pink with rage. 'I said I didn't want you here.'

'Right.' Lucas made his way to the door. 'I'll get off then. I'll come back tomorrow.'

'Don't bother.'

'Well I will. Happy Christmas Dad.'

Lucas leaned on the door outside his dad's rooms for a second. Carys, the young carer, was coming out of the room opposite. 'Are you okay?'

Lucas shrugged. 'He's not in a good mood today.'

The young girl smiled. 'Well a lot of people find Christmas difficult.'

'Yeah.'

'Maybe he'll be brighter tomorrow.'

Lucas stood up straight. 'Right. Well, I'd better get going. Are you working all day?'

She shook her head. 'Til four. We're going to have our dinner at tea time after I get off. My boyfriend's cooking it.' She pulled a face. 'I think it'll be okay.'

Lucas smiled properly. 'It sounds great.'

She nodded, and then paused. 'Look. It's not my place but . . . '

'But what?'

'Well, a lot of the people who live here, they're difficult. Brain injuries, mental health problems, addiction. It's no-one's fault but it's tough. Lots of the families don't visit that much. And that's okay. I mean maybe not okay, but nobody'd judge them.'

'You mean nobody would judge me?'

She nodded.

She was trying to be kind, but she was wrong. Someone would always judge Lucas. Lucas would always judge Lucas. He wished Carys a Merry Christmas and wandered back to his car. Carys was wrong about the rest of it too. Not about it being hard. Not about the fact that lots of families didn't visit that much. But about the fact that it was nobody's fault. He'd known, all those years ago, that his dad was drinking too much. He'd known that he was vulnerable, and he'd chosen to take a day off from the life he'd felt trapped in to piss about with a mate and go to a party and kiss a girl. The girl crystallised in his imagination. He could still see her perfectly in his head. Round face, button nose, bright blue eyes, blonde curls pulled back into a pony tail. He could remember her telling him about her parents and her school and her mates. He could remember her looking embarrassed at how lame it sounded, and he could remember being entranced by the sheer normality of her life and the sheer remarkableness of her. And that's what he'd been doing while his dad was drinking a whole bottle of whisky on top of a stomach full of pints and then taking a rental car for a spin across the north of England. It had been Lucas's unique situation that had given his dad the means to take that drive, and Lucas's lack of care that had given him the opportunity. Lucas wasn't like those other families who could decide to walk away, because what had happened to his dad really was his fault.

He drove back across the capital on autopilot, mentally taking Lucas off and putting Alan back on as he went. The lack of Christmas day traffic meant that the parking space outside the house was still empty. He pulled in and made his way inside. Trish and Charlie were in the kitchen, cheerfully bickering over a nut roast. Trish grinned as he came in. 'Charlie says her nut roast won't fit in the oven with your turkey.'

'Course it will.' Lucas got down on his hands and knees and opened the oven, pulling the turkey out and moving the shelves around until everything, just about, squeezed in. 'There you go.'

Charlie feigned a swoon. 'Oh Fake Alan. You're our hero.'

'Where's Cora?'

Trish frowned. 'Dunno. Still in bed?'

Lucas pulled potatoes and carrots out of the cupboard. 'I didn't hear her come in last night.'

Charlie grinned. 'I bet she's banging Santa.'

Lucas laughed. He hoped Charlie was right. He didn't know the details but he was pretty sure Cora was due some good luck in life. The house phone next to the front door rang. All three of them frowned. Who even knew their landline number? Lucas followed Charlie into the hallway and watched her tentatively lift the handset. She grinned and nodded. 'Okay . . . All right . . . Okay. See you then.' She hung up. 'That was Cora. Santa and Santa's whole family are coming for dinner.'

Lucas paused. They'd been planning a quiet dinner, just the four of them. That had seemed okay. He was going to be quietly at home. If he wasn't having too much fun, then it didn't need to make him feel any guiltier.

'What's up?' Trish leaned on the wall next to him.

He shook his head. He could hardly turn Santa away on Christmas Day. All he could do was make the best of things. 'Nothing. I guess I better do some more potatoes.'

Christmas Day, 2014

Jessica

Jess had walked a really long way. She wasn't sure how far, but the streets had started looking unfamiliar about an hour ago and she'd kept walking. Her phone had rung a lot, but she'd switched it to silent so it wasn't really bothering her anymore. The Baileys was three-quarters gone, but her head felt surprisingly clear, as if all the alcohol had done was take the edge off the anguish enough to bring her back into equilibrium. Everything was calm. All there was to think about was the walking.

Patrick's affair hadn't ended.

He'd promised her that it was over, but then she'd heard him promising that other woman, the perfect woman with the perfect hair, that he was going to end it with Jess and be with her. Both promises couldn't be true, could they? And there was no reason to expect him to break his promises to his perfect lover.

Jess kept walking.

She knew that she was probably supposed to be more upset than this. She remembered when she'd first found out about the affair back in September. It had all come out at Michelle and Sean's wedding. The shock had ripped through her whole body. She'd cried. She thought she might have shouted. There was none of that now. Maybe it was the drink, or maybe the horror was already out of her system. This was much better. This time she was going to deal with the whole thing maturely and calmly. She wasn't going to show herself up or make a scene.

Jess stopped walking and looked around. The Thames flowed alongside her and this part of the South Bank was lined with apartment buildings. So here she was. Of course. Where else could she possibly have been heading? She stepped up to the column of doorbells and pressed the button. A few seconds later the intercom crackled. A man's voice. That was odd. 'Who is it?'

Had she pressed the wrong buzzer? She checked again. The sub-penthouse bell was all lit up. 'Er . . . I'm here to see Cora.'

'What? Oh Miss Strachan? She moved out.'

'What? Where did she go?'

'Dunno. Sorry.' The intercom fizzled for a second and went quiet.

It shouldn't matter. Jess wasn't even sure why she'd come here. She didn't need to see Cora. She'd heard quite enough already from Patrick, but suddenly seeing Cora was the only thing that mattered. She had to confirm that it was true, and Patrick would lie. The realisation made her pause. It wasn't something she'd discovered today. She'd always known.She'd just never called it what it was before. He made big gestures and sweeping declarations. He bought her presents and whisked her away on exciting trips. She'd told herself that Patrick was romantic. Patrick was impulsive. Patrick didn't always remember details, but really Patrick lied.

It was part of who he was, but Cora might tell her the truth. Jess stared up at the apartment building as if the bricks and mortar might give a clue as to where she'd gone. And then she realised. Sean would know where Cora was. Or if he didn't know, he'd be able to find out. They'd been childhood sweethearts and next door neighbours. If he didn't know, then someone in his family would.

She pulled her phone from her pocket, ignored the flashing message notifications and phoned Michelle. Her friend was initially reluctant. Why did Jess need Cora's address? It was Christmas day. Was something wrong? Jess didn't intend to lie, but she wasn't ready to tell the truth. Michelle would worry, and that would spoil her Christmas, and that wouldn't be fair. So Jess told her friend that Christmas was a time for forgiveness, and she wanted to write a letter to Cora to get closure on the whole thing. And no, she didn't have to do it today, but if she didn't she might lose her nerve, so could Michelle please ask Sean or his mum if they had Cora's new address? Michelle agreed and a few minutes later a text arrived with the address.

Jess took a final big gulp from her bottle, tapped the postcode into her navigation app and set off walking again.

Christmas Day, 2014

Lucas

Lucas was enjoying himself. Despite his best efforts and his promise to himself that he would have a quiet Christmas, he was actually having fun. Cora had appeared with her department store Santa, whose real name turned out to be Liam, the Santa's brother and nephew and aunt. As they were piling the mountains of food on the table, Liam's flatmate turned up as well. They had a proper houseful, and Lucas had never experienced a Christmas Day like it. When he was little, Christmases had been low key affairs — usually just him and his dad. They might go and visit his grandparents, or even his mum, on Boxing Day but the family weren't particularly close. After everything changed there'd been

Christmases in swanky hotels, and at least one year on the beach in LA. There'd never been a big traditional Christmas dinner with family and friends. Lucas leant back and watched the room full of people talk and eat and joke. There was a pull of something in his chest. The feeling that this was the right place for him to be. The feeling that this was somewhere he belonged.

It wasn't a new feeling, but it was one he'd forgotten. It was the feeling he'd had as a kid on Saturday afternoons poring over comic books in the shop with his dad. It was the feeling he'd had at drama club, where his dad had sent him for two hours every Saturday morning. It was the feeling he thought he'd had for a moment in a kitchen at a Christmas party many years ago. And that was the last time. That was the last time that Lucas had even believed that it was possible to simply be himself.

After what seemed like several hours, people pushed chairs away from the table, and rubbed overfull bellies. Lucas started to clear the dishes as everyone agreed that they couldn't possibly eat another thing. A second later they were agreeing, just as loudly, that he could leave the cheese out. And the mints. But that would definitely be plenty.

Cora and Liam followed him into the kitchen. 'We'll wash up mate. We kinda overran your Christmas.'

Lucas shrugged. 'That's okay.' He started clearing up as Liam filled the sink and Cora hunted for a dry tea towel. 'So what do you do?'

Liam frowned. 'You don't recognise me?'

Lucas shook his head.

Cora laughed. 'Fake Alan doesn't read the tabloids.'

'Why do they call you Fake Alan?'

Lucas kept his mouth shut, and let Cora provide the answer. 'Because Alan's not his real name.'

Then it was time for Lucas to jump in and head off further questions. 'What have the tabloids got to do with anything?

Cora held up a tea towel of indeterminate cleanliness. 'Liam's an actor. He's been a bit torn apart by the papers lately.'

Lucas nodded. 'Right. That must be tough.' He couldn't say anything else. He felt as if his skin was burning red already. He couldn't say he knew how it felt.

At the sink Liam nodded. 'I'm getting through it.'

How? How do you get through it? How do you keep hold of who you are in the midst of notoriety? That was what Lucas wanted to ask. He didn't. The doorbell rang. Lucas grabbed the excuse to escape.

Somehow the conversation had got to him. He was remembering that Christmas Eve night fourteen years ago. The party. The crash. The girl. And then the papers afterwards. They'd vilified him. It sort of made sense. No-one could account for Lucas's whereabouts that day. Nobody had ever reported outright that he was driving, but the story of a mixed-up kid who'd gone off the rails was a familiar narrative and the papers had latched onto it. All because of that one night. The party. The crash.

He opened the door.

The girl.

5

Christmas Day, 2014

Jessica

Great, thought Jess. Another wrong address. The man on the doorstep was staring at her. He was good-looking with light brown stubble around his jaw, and bright green eyes that made Jess feel like she'd seen them somewhere before, and he was definitely staring at her. Jess had turned up on his doorstep on Christmas Day though — that was probably to be expected. Bodies appeared in the hallway behind him. None of them were Her. 'Does Cora live here?'

The man's jaw dropped open, but he didn't reply.

'Cora Strachan — is she here?'

Eventually the man nodded. 'Cora!'

She appeared from the end of the hallway, tea towel in hand, cheeks pink from the heat inside the flat, dark brown hair pulled up into a pony tail. She looked disappointingly normal. 'What?' She stopped as she saw Jess. 'Oh.'

This was the moment. This was what she'd walked across London for. This was her moment to find out the truth. Jess opened her mouth and wailed. She listened to her own wail. It wasn't what she'd expected. She didn't know how to make it stop. It was rising up from somewhere inside her chest and pushing its way out of her. She tried to swallow it down, but it bubbled up again, accompanied by a big gulping sob.

'Right.' The doorstep man put a hand under her elbow. 'Maybe you should sit down.'

She let him usher her, past Cora, and past a whole lot of other faces too, into a living room. She sat on the sofa and accepted glasses of water and offers of tissues. This wasn't right. Wasn't she supposed to be angry? She thought she probably was. She was a woman scorned. She'd intended to be calm, while channelling her fury in a controlled sort of a way. She wasn't supposed to be sitting on a sagging settee in the middle of somebody else's Christmas party blubbing uncontrollably.

She forced herself to look around. She'd been aware that it was Christmas Day, but somehow she'd still imagined Cora on her own in that perfect apartment. That was what other women did, wasn't it? They spent Christmas alone. They didn't have lives. They had affairs. In reality, her rival had a houseful of people. She had friends, and a tea towel. That seemed wrong. Mistresses weren't supposed to do the washing up. Jess looked around the room. Two women stood close together, holding hands and staring at her. Then there was doorstep man, and another guy the same age, and an older woman, and a man with a little boy. People were bustling around putting coats on and making excuses. 'You don't have to go on my account.'

The older woman nodded. 'You're all right pet. We've got to get back.' She looked around uncertainly. 'Well we'll leave you to it.'

That left the two women, the doorstep man, Cora and a blond guy who seemed to be hanging back. Cora sat down next to her. 'Why are you here Jessica?'

That was the question, wasn't it? Why was she here? She remembered. 'I know it's still going on.'

Cora frowned. 'What?'

'I know. You're still seeing my husband, aren't you?'

This time Cora exchanged a look with the blond man. 'I'm not. I promise you I'm not.' She was looking at the blond man, rather than at Jess now. 'I haven't seen him since the wedding.'

Jess shook her head. That wasn't

right. She'd heard him on the phone this morning to the woman he wanted to be with instead of Jess. 'I heard you. This morning.'

The blond man stepped forward. 'This morning?'

'Well lunchtime. I heard her on the phone to him.'

Cora was still shaking her head. The blond man put his hand on her shoulder. 'Cora's been with me all morning. Up until now.' He gestured around the room. 'At lunchtime we were all here together. I promise you. Whoever you heard on the phone, it wasn't her.'

That didn't make sense. Patrick had to have been talking to Cora. A glimmer of hope flickered to life on the horizon. If he really hadn't been talking to his lover then maybe Jess had misunderstood. Her husband's words from earlier in the day replayed in her head. *I'd rather be with you . . . After Christmas it'll be you and me. A fresh start . . . I love you babe.*

She closed her eyes and slumped back in the chair.

'Cora, can we have a word in the kitchen?' That must have been one of the women, and the question was followed by the sound of footsteps trooping away.

'I'll stay, and make sure she's okay.' Jess opened one eye. Doorstep man had sat himself down in the armchair next to the TV.

Jess opened the other eye and looked around the room. There were still cheese and biscuits on the dining table. Her stomach turned over unpleasantly. She'd walked out on her own dinner. Simon and her parents would be worried. She needed to look at her phone. Her phone was in her pocket. The effort of moving her arm, reaching into her pocket, switching on the screen was too much. She looked at the doorstep man again. His gaze was still fixed on her. 'Why are you staring at me?'

He opened his mouth.

Jess didn't need an answer. 'I've barged into your Christmas haven't I?' Somehow that hadn't seemed a bad idea at all while she was marching across the deserted streets of the capital, but this stranger was clearly horrified by her. 'I'm sorry. It's been a weird day.'

'I got that.'

'And I drank a whole bottle of Baileys.'

'Like a mini-bar bottle?'

Jess shook her head.

'Right. Okay. Well let me know if you're going to puke.'

'I'm not.' She closed her eyes again. 'I don't feel drunk. Just a bit numb.'

'That'll be shock. I'd offer you a whisky for it, but maybe not.'

Jess shrugged. 'I don't know how I got here.'

'No. I mean there's no tube today.'

'No! I know how I got *here*. I don't know how I got here in life. It was all going all right, you know. I've got a job. We managed to get a mortgage, just. And we had a lovely wedding.' She took a deep breath. 'It was last Christmas. And then she happened.'

Another surge of sadness hit Jess when she mentioned Cora. It felt good in a way. If she was feeling something, it meant she was still alive, somewhere inside the shell of Jess that was walking around and talking to people.

Doorstep man moved to sit next to her. 'Look. I've not known Cora that long, but I don't think she's been seeing anyone, and she was here at lunchtime with all of us.'

Jess looked properly at the stranger. Her gaze met his. Those bright green eyes. 'Do I know you?'

Christmas Day, 2014

Lucas

Lucas hesitated. He'd known the girl from the kitchen the second he'd opened the door. She looked, to his eyes at least, exactly the same. The same open face. The same bright blue eyes, but fourteen years, washing the dye out of his hair and growing a beard had clearly made him less recognisable. And what if that wasn't even what she was thinking of? What if she recognised him from somewhere else? He ignored the racing of his heart and shook his head. 'I don't think so.'

She frowned but didn't argue. She obviously had other things on her mind.

'I might go and see what the others are doing. Do you want anything? Water? Tea?'

The woman shook her head.

Lucas made his way into the kitchen. Cora was leaning on the worktop with a very large glass of wine in her hand, and Liam's arm around her shoulders. Trish and Charlie were casting anxious glances towards the lounge.

'Is she okay?'

Lucas nodded. 'I think so. Will someone tell me what's going on?'

Cora sighed.

'The short version.'

The short version was surprisingly short. Cora had had an affair with the woman's husband. Cora definitely had not known he was married, and had definitely ended things as soon as she'd found out. The woman seemed to be under the impression that her husband was still seeing someone, but that someone was not Cora.

Poor girl from the kitchen.

Trish cleared her throat. 'So what are we going to do with her?'

Cora took a glug of wine. 'Well I don't see why she's our responsibility.'

Lucas thought back over his meal. One glass of wine. Nothing before that because he'd driven to and from his dad's. Then he thought about the woman. He should let her walk away. He didn't need ghosts from the past. 'I could give her a lift home?'

Trish shrugged. 'Is she going to want to go home?'

A cough from the doorway inter- rupted the conversation. 'A lift would be very kind. Thank you. I walked here, and I'm not entirely clear on the way home.'

Charlie boggled. 'You walked here? Where do you live?'

She gave them an address a long way south of the river.

'But that's like what? Two hours? I don't even know.'

The woman nodded. 'Sorry to have interrupted your day.'

Lucas led the way to his car, and waited for her to get in.

'It's nice of you to take me home.'

'It's fine.'

'Why are you being so nice to me? I ruined your day.'

'It's just a lift.' That wasn't a reason. The reason was that he didn't want to let her go yet. She was the girl from the kitchen. She was from the time before everything in the world had gone wrong. Kissing her was probably the last good thing he'd done. However much his head told him to steer clear, something else was making him want to eke out every available second in her company. That wasn't the only thing though. 'It looked like you were having a crap time. I know what that's like, when everything falls apart.' He paused. He wasn't sure what to say that would help her. 'Look. If you don't mind me saying, you seem very calm.'

'What do you mean?'

'Well if my husband . . . ' That didn't sound right. ' . . . or wife, or whatever was having an affair I'd be furious. Why aren't you throwing his stuff out of an upstairs window? Or cutting his suits up? Or whatever it is that wronged women do?'

'I don't know.' Lucas let her think about it for a moment. 'I'm numb. I was devastated the first time, when I found out about Cora. This time, it's more like I've been waiting for the axe to fall and now it has. And there's no point getting angry.'

It seemed to Lucas that there was every point, but it wasn't his place to say. 'So what are you going to do?'

'I have no idea.' She fell silent for a

second. Lucas tried to concentrate on driving rather than the thoughts that were crashing around his head. The girl from the kitchen had walked back into his life, onto his doorstep. The younger Lucas would have thought that was fate, but he wasn't that boy anymore. And, he reminded himself, she wasn't that girl. She was married. Whatever was going on there, that fact remained, she was married. Her voice interrupted his train of thought. 'Talk to me about something.'

'About what?'

'Anything. Distract me.' She sighed. 'What's your favourite bit of Christmas?'

Lucas didn't know how to answer that. 'Christmas was never really a big deal when I was a kid. It was just me and my dad, so it was kinda low key.'

She frowned. 'Was your dad there today?'

Lucas shook his head. 'He's not very well. He lives in a care home.'

'Sorry.'

'It's okay.'

'I used to love the romance of Christmas.'

'The romance?'

'The magic of it, you know. I actually had my first kiss on Christmas Eve.'

Lucas glanced across at his passenger. She was turned away from him, staring out of the window. Did she know? 'Really?'

'Yeah. Long time ago though. Never saw him again.' She laughed a brittle little laugh. 'And I got married at Christmas, so maybe I'm better off not believing in romantic Christmas miracles, because they really don't last.'

'I'm sure he had a reason.'

'He'll have a hundred reasons. He always does.'

Lucas stopped. She meant her husband. Of course she did. She wasn't thinking about some kid she'd snogged half a lifetime ago. 'I meant the first kiss boy.'

'Reasons for what?'

'Not getting in touch.'

'You don't have to be nice. He didn't call because he didn't fancy me. Like my first boyfriend at university forgot to tell me he was gay because he didn't really care about me. Like Patrick cheats because he doesn't really love me. It's not them, is it? It can't be all the men. It must be me.'

Lucas didn't know what to say. If he told her would it lay one tiny ghost to rest or would it make her hate him forever?

'It's left here.'

'What?'

'Left at these lights.'

Lucas followed her directions for the rest of the journey and pulled up outside an uninspiring modern block of flats.

'They used to be council, but it was what we could afford.'

'I'm sure they're great inside.'

She shook her head. 'Not really.' She twisted in her seat to look at him properly. 'I don't want to go in.'

'Do you want me to come with you?'

'I can't ask you to do that.'

'I don't mind.'

'No. I have to deal with it, don't I?' She was still staring at his face. 'Are you sure we don't know each other?'

This was the moment. She'd asked twice now, and she'd explicitly mentioned the kiss. Before he could have pretended not to recognise her. Now he really had to say something. His phone played the theme from *Star Wars* in his pocket. 'Sorry.' The screen showed *Morning Rise Care*. 'It's my dad's home. I'm sorry.'

She nodded. 'It's fine.'

He watched her getting out of the car. She walked up the path and then paused. The phone was still ringing. He hit answer and spoke into the phone. 'Hold on a second.'

Lucas jumped out of the car, rummaging through his pockets for a bit of paper. He found an old receipt. Wait. No pen. Back in the car and he pulled stuff out of the glove box. A tiny length of pencil. It would do. He scrawled his number on the receipt and handed it solemnly to the girl from the kitchen. 'Let me know you're okay. Or not. If you need anything, you can give me a call.'

She nodded. 'You're really very kind.'

Lucas shrugged. 'Not really.' He glanced down at the phone in his hand. To call on Christmas Day afternoon it must be some sort of crisis. 'I really have to go.'

He strode back to the car, jumped into the driver's seat and lifted the phone back to his ear. 'Sorry. What's the problem?'

6

Christmas Day, 2014

Jessica

She watched the guy from the doorstep drive away, and realised that she hadn't even asked his name. Another man choosing to walk — or in this case drive — away from her. She looked at the scrap of paper he'd given her. She wasn't going to call him. He was just being kind. She'd probably throw it away. She folded the tiny piece of paper carefully and pushed it deep into her pocket.

So there was nothing else for it. It was time to go inside and face the rest of her life. She headed up the stairs to the flat, and opened the door tentatively. 'Hello?'

'In here.' The voice came from the living room. It wasn't Patrick.

'Simon?' Her brother was sitting on his own flicking through a magazine. 'Where is everyone?'

'I gave mum and dad the keys to my place. They're going to stay there.'

Jess nodded. She couldn't pretend she wasn't relieved. 'Are they cross with me?'

Simon hesitated. 'They didn't really say anything.'

That figured. Jess's parents weren't people who liked to cause a stir.

'And Patrick?'

'I asked Patrick to leave.'

'Why?'

'Why do you think?'

'He told you?'

Simon raised an eyebrow. 'I didn't give him much choice.'

'You didn't hit him, did you?'

Her brother shook his head. 'I didn't hit him. I should have hit him.'

Jess sat down. 'What did he tell you?'

'Not much. Stuff you already know, I guess.'

Jess hesitated. She didn't actually know very much. 'Tell me anyway.'

'Well, when you disappeared I looked all around the flat for you, and then outside and then I checked with your neighbours, and nobody had seen anything. And then Patrick said, 'She must have heard me . . . ' I don't think he realised anyone was listening, but I was, so I made him tell me what you heard.'

'Him on the phone?'

Simon nodded. 'To this new girlfriend of his.'

New girlfriend? So Cora had been telling the truth. Jess closed her eyes. 'It's definitely somebody new?'

'He said he'd met her in November. He said that he couldn't help who he fell in love with.'

Love? Patrick had mentioned love on the phone, but it hadn't really sunk in. Her husband loved somebody else. Well that was probably final then wasn't it? 'Did he say anything about her?'

Simon shook his head. 'She's called Vicky.'

'Right.' Jess wasn't sure what she'd

been expecting when she got home. Probably some sort of emotional scene. Even in her head that idea looked more like a soap opera than real life. She could picture the soap opera Jess shouting and throwing crockery across the room. She couldn't quite imagine doing it herself.

'Where have you been all day?'

'I went to see Cora.'

Simon raised a questioning eyebrow.

'The last one. I thought it was her again.'

'He says it's not.'

'No.' Jess looked around the room. 'You've cleared up.'

'Yeah.'

'Thank you.' She paused. 'And thank you for sorting mum and dad, and dealing with Patrick. So he's gone to hers? To this Vicky person's house.'

Simon nodded. 'I guess so. He said to ask you to call him. I promised I would.'

'Do you think I should?'

Simon didn't answer straight away. 'I told him I'd pass on the message. Jessie, it can't be up to me what you do now.'

Jess nodded. He was right. It wasn't up to Simon what happened next. It wasn't really up to Jess. All the decisions were Patrick's now, and he seemed to have decided to love someone else. Jess just had to go along with things. 'I'm tired. I'm really really tired.'

'I'm not surprised. Do you want me to stay tonight?'

He could. The spare room was already made up. Jess shook her head. 'I'm okay on my own.'

'Are you?'

She nodded. 'I'm going to have to be.'

She walked into the hallway with her brother, and let him hug her on the doorstep. 'Jessie . . . '

'What?'

Her brother shook his head. 'It's not my place . . . No. Sorry. I shouldn't tell you what to do.'

'What?'

Her brother stared down at the floor and answered in a whisper. 'Just don't take him back this time.'

Jess swallowed. Of course she wasn't

going to take him back. It didn't sound like she was going to get the chance.

Boxing Day, 2014

Lucas

For a brief moment it had been the best of Christmases, but then it had been the worst. Well not the worst. That title had been wrapped up fourteen years ago, but it had been pretty awful. Lucas leant back against the wall in the hospital and rubbed his back. Hospital waiting rooms hadn't got any more comfortable in the last decade and a half.

A nurse cleared her throat somewhere near his right elbow. 'Er . . . Mr Woods? Your father is awake. He seems quite well, if you want to see him.'

Lucas nodded. 'Will you be discharging him?'

The nurse paused. 'We're waiting for the consultant. We need to evaluate your father's mental state.'

Lucas shook his head. 'Well he has a

95

brain injury. The carer said she'd explained all that last night.'

'Maybe you should speak to the consultant.'

'I'm speaking to you.' The edge of frustration that Lucas tried so hard to avoid was there in his voice.

'Right. Well, we need to establish whether your father's overdose was accidental.'

Well no. Obviously. You couldn't secretly keep half of your pills for six months under the noses of a building full of trained carers by accident. But somehow Lucas had mentally filed it as another crazy thing his dad had done. 'You mean you think he was trying to kill himself?'

'It's difficult with your father's other conditions. It might not even be something he'd thought out to that extent.' She paused. 'That's what the consultant will be trying to establish.'

Lucas slumped back into the chair. His poor dad. Lucas had been too busy feeling sorry for himself, hadn't he? He hadn't thought about what his dad was going through all this time. He swallowed down the guilt as best he could. He could make this better. Things could change. He could change them. He'd find his own place, somewhere where his dad could live with him this time. He had to take responsibility properly. He'd been pretending, trying to live half a life out there in the world, rather than really dealing with what he'd done to his dad.

He took a deep breath and took the short walk into the ward. There were six beds, separated by curtains. Two were empty — Lucas guessed that all the non-urgent patients got sent home before Christmas. The others were occupied by thin white-haired men, dozing, heads lolling on their pillows. His dad's bed was at the farthest end of the room, next to the window. His father was sitting up in bed looking around eagerly. 'Lukey! Is it Christmas Day yet?'

Lucas shook his head. 'It was Christmas Day yesterday, Dad. It's Boxing Day now.'

His father frowned. 'Did I get my presents already?'

Lucas nodded. 'You did. You had a selection box, and some socks and a comic book.'

The older man's eyes lit up. 'Avengers?'

'Avengers.'

'Who's your favourite Avenger Lukey?'

'Iron Man.' It had always been Iron Man. Thor was a god. Captain America sort of had stuff done to him. The Hulk was out of control. Tony Stark had decided what he wanted to be. He'd planned and worked and designed. His superpowers weren't the result of a freak accident. Iron Man made it seem like it might be possible to be in control of your own life. It was a fantasy, obviously, but it was a good one.

'I like Thor.'

'Thor's cool too . . . Dad, do you remember yesterday you took some pills?'

His dad pulled a face. 'I take pills every day.'

'But yesterday you took more.'

'Will you bring my comic books in Lukey?'

Lucas nodded. 'Sure.'

The nurse appeared at the end of the bed. 'Sorry Mr Woods. It's not officially visiting time at the moment. It'll be breakfast soon and then the consultant should be round.'

'Okay.' He peered at his dad. 'I've got to go for a bit. This lady is going to look after you. They're going to bring you breakfast.'

'Cornflakes?'

Lucas glanced at the nurse. 'Of course.'

His dad seemed quite happy. That was definitely getting rarer, but at least it meant that Lucas could leave him for a couple of hours without worrying about coming back to stories of him trying to punch a nurse or get out of bed and make a run for the nearest off licence.

He rubbed his eyes as he waited for the lift. He'd barely slept in the plastic waiting room chair, and every time he'd started to drop off he'd been woken up by a nurse telling him he didn't need to stay overnight. He needed caffeine, and then he needed to go to the care home and pick up some stuff, and then . . . and then what? It was Boxing Day. Could he really get things moving on Boxing Day?

He ordered a double espresso and

found a seat in the corner of the hospital coffee shop. He didn't want to put things off any longer. If he waited, he'd persuade himself that how things were at the moment was good enough. And besides, he'd called this long-time solicitor on Christmas morning back when his dad had had the actual accident. Boxing Day was quite civilised by comparison. He scrolled through his phone until he found the number of Mr Daley of Daley, Callendar & Associates, and let his finger hover for a second over the 'Call' button. And then his phone rang. The incongruity made him pause. *Unknown Number*. Normally he didn't even answer those, but it wouldn't be a sales call on Boxing Day, would it?

Boxing Day, 2014

Jessica

This was a mistake. She should be ringing Simon or Michelle. They always knew what to do. They always knew when she was taking a wrong turn. She made a deal with herself. If he didn't pick up in five rings, then she'd hang up. One ring.

He'd probably be freaked out to hear from her anyway. He'd clearly only given her his number out of pity.

Two rings.

Michelle would tell her that the last thing she needed was some random bloke hanging around.

Three rings.

Simon would add that she needed to resolve things with Patrick. Maybe she should be calling him.

Four rings.

Jess's mother would mutter something about Jess needing to pull her socks up a bit around the house.

Five rings.

She moved her finger to the 'End call' icon.

'Hello.'

'Hi. Is that . . . ' She stopped. She didn't even know his name. 'I mean, this is Jessica.'

'Jessica?'

And he wouldn't remember hers, would he? 'Jess. From yesterday. The crazy woman.'

She could hear the smile in his voice. 'What's up Jess?'

Such a simple question. 'Well my husband's having an affair. His second affair in about six months. In fact I think he's left me for her. I guess it's not actually an affair if he really does leave his wife is it? It's like she's his girlfriend now. That must make me the other woman.' Her words came out in a torrent, and she was giggling as she spoke, which was strange because nothing she was saying was funny, but now she'd started the laughter didn't seem to want to subside.

'I'm sorry.'

'It's fine.'

'No. It's not. It's shit.'

She stopped laughing. He was right. That was exactly what it was.

'What can I do?'

She took a deep breath. 'I need someone to help me find him.'

'Are you sure?'

'Absolutely.'

'Okay, well I understand if you want to have it out with him.' He paused. 'Am I the best person though? I mean, don't you have friends you can ask?'

Of course he didn't want to help. Why would he? She was a stranger. 'Right. Yeah. Sorry. I don't know what I was thinking.' Jess pulled her phone away from her ear and hit 'End Call.' A second later it rang again.

'Hello?'

'I didn't mean I wouldn't help. Of course I'll help.'

Jess didn't know what to say.

'Right. I've got to do one thing, and then I'll come over there?'

'Thank you.'

'Give me an hour.'

That gave Jess an hour to work out where on earth Patrick actually was. She couldn't very well ask . . . she swore under her breath — she still didn't know his name . . . but she still couldn't very well ask him to drive around London looking for a house that looked like a whore might live there. But how did you go about finding a missing husband?

She could phone him and ask, but that would mean talking to him now, and if she talked to him now she might lose her nerve for the talking to him face-to-face she needed to do later. She'd had all night to think about everything. All night lying in bed staring at the wall, waiting for morning, to decide that she needed to talk to Patrick face-to-face. She needed to know for herself what was going on. If it was over, if he was never coming back, she needed to hear that from him.

So she wouldn't phone him. What then? She tried Facebook, but it was too much to hope that he'd tagged his location in the last twenty hours. She paused. That wasn't the only thing that Facebook could tell her though, was it? She swiped and clicked her way to his friend list and scrolled down. Vicky? Simon had said her name was Vicky.

Amongst Patrick's two hundred friends there were two Victorias. One Jess recognised. She'd been at the wedding, and was, apparently, happily married and living in Alicante. She seemed unlikely. The other Victoria was unfamiliar. Jess clicked on the name. She was beautiful. Smooth dark brown skin, and super-short buzz cut hair. You had to have an amazing face to wear your hair that short, and this woman did. She looked like Grace Jones and Beyonce had got together and made an even more luminous daughter.

The voice in Jess's head told her that she ought to stop looking. Victoria (Vix) Morris's timeline was a cascade of beautiful people having tremendous times. From November, there were photos of champagne on a roof garden with views across the city. Two glasses of champagne, Jess noted. From December there was a selfie of Victoria in a bodycon tube dress and heels captioned 'On the way to meet my boy #datenight.' From Christmas Eve a single status update

'Totally can't believe some women. Would never get all clingy and nagging around my man. Have some self-respect sisters.'

My man. But he wasn't Victoria's man. At least he wasn't supposed to be. He was supposed to be Jess's man. That's what he'd promised. He'd hired a suit and bought her a ring and stood up in front of all those people and promised that he loved her. He'd promised, explicitly, that he wasn't going to do this. Jess had meant it when she'd promised. She'd thought that she was sorted now. No more horrible dates. No more first kisses or first times going back to his place. No more dissatisfying first shags. She was done. She was his and he was hers. Only now he was Victoria's.

Jess sat down on the floor, in the middle of the hallway of the flat she'd bought with the husband she loved, and waited. Every inch of her body was on the brink of breaking down. She could feel the tears building behind her eyes, pressing for release, but refusing to fall.

She was stuck somewhere in between, not quite together but not even managing to properly fall apart.

7

Boxing Day, 2014

Lucas

Jessica. Lucas remembered the name from that night in the kitchen, but somehow it had never stuck in his imagination. She's always been the girl from the kitchen to him, but as he hadn't explained that to her, it was probably easier to try to get used to using her name. And he'd promised to help her this morning, and he'd promised his dad he'd be back in a couple of hours. The voice in Lucas's head pointed out that he couldn't fix everything, or everyone. Lucas ignored the voice. His dad was quite safe in hospital for now, and they knew not to discharge him unless it was to Lucas or the home's care, so he had plenty of time to help Jessica. He was being a Good Samaritan. That was all.

Everything in his dad's rooms was stored in drawers and cupboards marked with stickers saying what was inside, so it hadn't taken long to gather together a couple of comic books, some toiletries, pyjamas and a change of clothes. Half an hour later he was pulling up outside Jess's front door. He slipped in as a neighbour was coming out, took the stairs two at a time, and then stopped. He didn't know which flat she was in, did he? Shaking his head, Lucas pulled his phone from his pocket and rang the last number again. 'Hi. I'm in your building, but I don't know which flat it is.'

'Oh God! Sorry. I should have said.' He could hear her moving around through the phone, and a second later a door on the landing next to him opened. 'I'm coming to the door. I — '

She stopped as she saw him. Lucas waved awkwardly. 'Hi.'

'Hi.' The jolt of emotion he'd felt when he'd opened the door on Christmas Day punched him in the gut once again. Good Samaritan, he reminded himself. She needed support, not complications. 'How are you getting on?'

She shrugged. 'Thanks for coming. I don't know why I called you really. It's just . . . '

'Just what?'

She shrugged. 'I don't know. Sometimes things are easier with strangers.'

Lucas followed Jess into the flat. That was it. He was a stranger. He could understand that. Once people knew too many facts about you they started thinking they knew who you were. Anonymity was easier. It meant you could just be. 'So what's the plan?'

'Well I think I know who the other woman is, but I don't know where she lives, so we need to find that out.'

'Okay. And then what?'

'Then we're going to go around there.'

Lucas raised an eyebrow.

'I need to see him. Even if it's horrible news, I need to hear it from him.'

Even if it's horrible news? Lucas

wondered for a second what sort of non-horrible news she was hoping for. He stopped himself. He knew what a seductive drug hope could be. 'So why do you need me?'

She sighed. 'I was hoping you could drive me. Patrick took our car. My car. Patrick took my car.'

So he was the chauffeur for a woman who clearly wanted her cheating husband back. The feeling in his gut fizzled away. 'Right then. You don't know where she lives?'

Jess shook her head. 'Just a name. It's hopeless isn't it?'

Lucas frowned. The internet had really wreaked havoc with people's ability to think. 'Have you looked her up in the phone book?'

Boxing Day, 2014

Jessica

She hadn't looked her up in the phone book. She didn't even know the phone

111

book was still a thing. 'I don't know if we've got one.'

'Everyone's got one. It'll be on a shelf or in a drawer under your landline phone.'

Jess shook her head. The landline was on top of the little table in the hallway. She turned to check. There was nothing underneath except a pile of takeaway menus and junk mail that neither of them had got around to throwing away, and ... and a phone book. 'Wow. You're a phone book savant.'

He moved past her and picked the book up from the floor. 'So what's her surname?'

'Morris.'

'M-O-R-R-I-S?'

Jess nodded, and watched him flick through the pages.

'There's two V Morrises.' He showed her the page.

'So how do we tell which it is?'

He shrugged. 'What else do you know about her?'

'Not much. Does it say that either of them's a husband stealing whore?'

'Strangely no.'

'Okay.' Jess flicked back to Victoria's Facebook profile. 'She checked in at South Kensington Tube on 22nd December, and twice at places on Gloucester Road the week before.'

'Hold on. I think one of these is near South Ken.' She watched while he got his own phone out and tapped an address in. 'Yep. Well it's not much, but I guess she's our best bet.'

Jess nodded. This was it then. They had a name. They had a probable address. She had a willing chauffeur. There was no reason not to go around there and have it out. 'Do you think I should take some of Patrick's things?'

He shrugged. 'Well if it's definitely over it would save you having to see him here again, I guess.'

Jess looked around the flat. Beyond clothes she wasn't sure what was really his and what was hers. There was the mirror in the hallway that his dad had made for them, which should make it Patrick's, but he'd made it to Jess's specification, so she didn't really know. There were the four good dining chairs which they'd bought together, but which had replaced four chairs Patrick had had in his old flat. So did they get two each? Then there were the wedding presents. They had a fondue set that had never been taken out of the box. Was it too late to send it back? Or would everyone want their pressies back? How long did you have to stay married to be allowed to keep the gifts?

She shook her head. 'I'll worry about his stuff later.'

In the car she wondered again if she should have more of a plan. 'What am I going to say to him?'

'What do you want to say?'

'I want to ask him what's going on.'

'Will he tell you?'

Jess didn't answer. Patrick was good with words. He'd been good with words in September when she'd found out about his thing with Cora. Was there a part of her that wanted him to be good with words now? Was there a part of her

114

that wanted him to find the thing to say that would make everything all right? Maybe if she was willing to take him back, if she opened up her heart a fraction, then he'd be able to find the perfect thing to say to make her believe that he could be happy with her. That wasn't what she was supposed to be hoping for. She was supposed to be angry. She was supposed to be full of fury and rage. She was supposed to know that she was the wronged woman, and that he had no right to expect her to take him back. That was what Simon would tell her. That was definitely what Michelle would tell her. She hadn't phoned either of them.

'So this is it.' He found a parking space and the two of them wandered along the street. 'It's 17a, so I guess it's above one of these shops.' They came to a stop in front of a florist. He nodded. 'Here. Are you ready?'

Jess shook her head. It felt very final. Before, when she'd tracked Cora down, she was relying on someone outside of her and Patrick to do something or to tell her something. This time it was just her and him. If they couldn't work it out, that would be it. She forced air into her lungs. 'All right then.'

The buzzer light flickered and a crackling female voice came through. 'It's open. Come up.'

'Guess they're expecting someone?' suggested Jess.

'Maybe. Remember this might not be the right V Morris. Do you want me to wait down here?'

Jess didn't. She wanted him to come with her and stand close enough to catch her if she fell down into a faint. 'Okay.'

The stairwell was dark and smelt of mould. At the top of the stairs a door was being flung open. 'Mum!' He stopped, stared at Jess, and folded his arms. Patrick. 'How did you find me Jessie?'

Jess didn't answer straight away. He'd said 'mum.' That must mean that her in-laws knew about this woman. Was she simply a laughing stock for his whole family? 'Hello Patrick.'

'Seriously, how did you find me?'

Jess shrugged. 'Facebook and the phone book.'

'Right. Cool.' He shuffled his feet. 'You probably shouldn't be here.'

She wasn't sure what she'd been expecting. Even in her fantasies he hadn't quite run into her arms declaring that he'd made a terrible mistake and begging her to take him back. At best he'd sort of assumed she would take him back, and Jess hadn't argued. It didn't seem like things were going that way.

'I wanted to see you.'

He rolled his eyes. 'Why?'

'To see what's going on. Simon said you admitted you were having an affair.'

Patrick shook his head. 'Come on Jessie.' He raised his fingers to make air quotes. 'An affair? We both know that us isn't working.'

'We've only been married a year.'

'Yeah. Since you finally decided I was worthy.'

That wasn't right. 'What do you mean?'

'Oh come on. How many times did I suggest moving in together or getting married?'

Jess shook her head, indignation rising from her gut. So what if the timing hadn't been right before? She swallowed back the impending tears. 'But we're married now.'

'Look, I am sorry.' He tilted his head and his eyes glinted in the light. 'Part of me will always love you, you know.'

'So we can . . . '

A voice called out from inside the flat. 'Is that your mum and dad, hon?'

Patrick looked over his shoulder. 'No. It's Jessica.'

'Really?' Now the voice sounded excited. Footsteps made a rapid stomping noise and then a second face appeared in the doorway gawping down at her. 'Wow. That's the sweetest thing. Has she come to win you back?'

None of this was going the way that Jess had thought, but somehow it was all entirely right. She hadn't deserved

118

him. She had been slow to commit, and now she was the naïve little girl who didn't understand. Patrick and Victoria were the grown-ups who thought everything she did was the sweetest thing. Sweet. Dull. Not sexy. Not smart. Not intoxicating like the woman who was currently snaking a perfectly toned arm around Jess's husband's torso. 'Right then. Well I'll go then.'

Patrick nodded. 'I think you should.'

The buzz of the intercom sounded. The other woman — this Victoria — ducked back into the flat. A second later she reappeared. 'Your parents are on their way up.'

Patrick looked down at Jess. 'You should go. You don't want to embarrass yourself.'

No. Of course she didn't, but it was too late now, wasn't it? They were already laughing at her, and she could hear footsteps at the bottom of the stairs. She was trapped. A second later Patrick's mother turned the corner, closely followed by his dad. Jess had always felt out of her depth with Patrick's parents. They were rich, which was one thing, but they weren't like Jess imagined rich people being. They exuded an air of worldliness. Patrick's mother threw her arms around Jess. 'Jessica, I didn't know you were going to be here.'

'I'm going.'

Patrick's mother shook her head. 'Oh, I do hope you weren't making a fool of yourself darling.'

All at once Jess found that her whole body felt out of shape. This always happened around Patrick's mother. It was as if the older woman's ease overwhelmed her and made everything about Jess feel awkward by comparison.

'I mean, things clearly weren't working out with you two, were they? And young people don't really accept the paradigm of traditional marriage anymore, do they?'

'I have to go.' It was all she could do. She couldn't stand here and make chit-chat about the outmoded construct of marriage. She couldn't persuade Patrick to change his mind. She needed to be somewhere else.

Patrick's voice carried down the stairs behind her. 'Are you going to bring my stuff over?'

Jess kept walking. Footsteps followed her down the stairs. 'Jessica!'

She stopped. It was Patrick's dad. He was a quiet man, usually found standing a few paces behind his wife. 'Look. I know you probably don't want to talk to me at the moment, but are you all right?'

She shrugged.

'Right. Well you will get through this. Just don't . . . ' he hesitated.

'What?'

'I know he's my son and everything, but promise me you won't take him back.'

'I know. You don't think I'm right for him.'

The older man shook his head. 'No. I meant for your sake.'

Boxing Day, 2014

Lucas

Lucas leant on the car and waited. What did a person say to their husband and his new lover, he wondered. And how long did it take? Was she going to be invited in for coffee and mince pies? It didn't take long to get an answer. Apparently not. Jess shot out of the door to the flats and straight back into the car.

'How did it go?'

'I don't want to talk about it.'

'Okay.' Whatever had happened clearly hadn't been what she was hoping for. 'What do you want to do?'

She sat very still for a moment. 'I'm not sure.'

'If you wanna talk about it . . . '

She stared away from him out of the window. 'There's nothing to tell.'

'You didn't punch him or anything? Or punch her?'

She shook her head. 'No. Do you think I should have?'

'I think he probably deserved it.' She

122

didn't reply. 'You're very calm again.'

She turned back towards him. 'Well what would getting upset solve?'

Lucas didn't reply. Getting upset didn't solve anything, but it was what people did. They cried and shouted and complained, and Lucas listened and advised and made things right again. 'Is there anything I can do?'

'I think I probably need to get my car back.'

It wasn't the answer he was expecting, but it was something they could actually do. 'Okay.'

'Unless you don't think that's fair? I mean I think I'm getting to keep the flat. Should I let him have the car?'

Lucas stared at her in disbelief. 'You found out he was shagging around on Christmas Day. I don't think you have to let him keep his bollocks if you don't want to.'

'Right.' She peered up the street in front of them. 'I can't see it.'

'What sort of car is it?'

'Silver 206.'

Lucas drove slowly around the streets near the flat, scanning the rows of parked cars as he went.

'Wait! There.' Jess was pointing across the road.

He pulled in and followed her across the street to her own car. She giggled awkwardly. 'Well then . . . '

She had her car back. That meant she didn't need him to drive her around. It meant he had no reason not to get back to the hospital. 'I guess I'll let you get on.'

'Right. You too.' She paused. 'Thank you. For today. And last night.'

'It's fine.' He wasn't sure what else to say. He couldn't tell her that he thought, no he knew, that he'd kissed her once years and years ago. He couldn't tell her that she was beautiful and whatever this Patrick guy thought was better in some dingy flat above a florist couldn't possibly be even a fraction as incredible as Jess herself. Saying any of that would lead to questions that Lucas wasn't ready to answer. 'I probably should go. My dad's in hospital, so . . . '

Her hand flew up to her mouth. 'Oh my god. Why didn't you say? You shouldn't have been running around after me all morning.'

'It's fine. I wanted to help.'

'Well, thank you.' She turned away and opened the car door. 'Wait. I never asked your name.'

'No. Right.' Lucas paused. Suddenly he didn't want to lie. 'People call me Alan.'

She frowned and stared into his face just for a second.

He dropped his gaze to the floor.

'People call you Alan? So that's your name?'

'Not exactly.' This was another moment. He could do it right now. He could say, 'My name is Lucas and we've actually met before,' but if he did that then it was only a matter of time before she knew everything. 'It's kind of a long story.'

She shook her head. 'Well bye then, People-call-you-Alan.'

'Bye Jess.' He stood back on the pavement and watched her drive away. So that was that. It was for the best. They both had far too many other things on their minds to rake over a moment from years ago.

He made his way back to the hospital. The ward was busier now. It was regular visiting hours and the other occupied beds in the bay had people sitting around them chatting to the patients. Lucas was surprised to find his own dad asleep. He sat down in the chair next to the bed and waited. After a few minutes a tall, young man appeared at the foot of the bed. 'I'm Mr Herrera. Are you Mr Woods?'

Lucas nodded. 'You're the consultant.'

'That's right. I wondered if I could have a quick word.'

Lucas followed the man past the nurses' station and into a consulting room.

'Unfortunately we did have to sedate your father after you went. He was distressed and aggressive.'

Lucas dropped his gaze to the floor. 'I'm sorry. It's since the brain injury. He doesn't . . . '

The consultant held up a hand. 'I understand your father's condition. Problems with impulse control, short and medium term memory loss, increased aggression?'

Lucas nodded.

'And I also understand that he is an alcoholic?'

Lucas nodded again.

'And that pre-dates the brain injury?'

Another nod.

'Okay.' It was that annoying doctor's 'okay', the one that implied that things weren't okay at all. 'And your father lives at Morning Rise?'

'Yeah.'

Lucas saw the slight flick of the eyebrow. Morning Rise was expensive. Lucas was aware that he didn't look like a man who'd be able to afford it. 'But I'm going to move him in with me. He'll be a lot better if he's with me.'

The consultant frowned. 'Well that is your decision.'

'Yes. It is.'

The man half-smiled. 'Of course. I do have to say though that it would seem to me that your father needs long-term professional care. His problems aren't simply physical.'

'I know that.' Lucas could hear the defensiveness in his own voice. Of course he knew what his dad's problems were. He'd been living with them for half his life. 'But I'm responsible for him, aren't I?'

The consultant frowned. 'You were sixteen when he had the accident?'

Lucas nodded.

'Look. I don't know you, and I don't know your situation, but let me tell you what I do know about young carers, not all of them, just some of those I've seen. When you're only a kid yourself and you find yourself caring for a parent, it's very easy to take on too much responsibility. You assume that everything is down to you somehow. It isn't. And for your dad, Morning Rise is probably one of the best places he could possibly be.'

'But . . .'

The man held up his hand. 'As I say, it's your decision, but your father's underlying condition isn't likely to improve significantly. It might be managed more or less effectively, but you understand that he isn't going to recover?'

Lucas didn't reply.

'Look, what I always say to families in this sort of situation is this. Make sure you're thinking about what's best for the patient, not what's going to make you feel better.'

Lucas stormed out of the consulting room. Presumptuous idiot. What did he know about Lucas's life? The thought stopped him short. What did anyone know about Lucas's life? His closest friends were his housemates, and all they knew was that he wasn't really called Alan. He'd never had a girlfriend who'd lasted more than a few weeks. It was hard to keep things going beyond the third or fourth date when all your anecdotes about your childhood stop aged ten, and you couldn't tell them who you really were. The only person who knew who he really was was his dad, and some days his dad barely recognised Lucas at all. He was a ghost, living half a life out here in the world, while the real Lucas drifted away into the ether. He sat down again next to his dad's bed, and watched the man sleep. He looked peaceful.

Lucas swallowed back the beginnings of a tear. He couldn't remember his dad ever looking peaceful. Before the accident he was always bouncing off the walls, buzzing over the next excitement. Even before everything changed he remembered his father as a restless soul. There'd been one day when Lucas had arrived home from school and found all the dining room furniture laid out on the lawn, and his dad with a paintbrush in hand, painting rainbow colours across the table top. Another time he'd set out to build a play house, but he'd run out of wood part way through. Lucas frowned as he remembered the other side of his dad's restlessness, the inability to stop after just one drink, the money lost in the pub or at the bookies, the tension he'd felt when he was the last child to be collected from the playground wondering if this was the day when his father wouldn't come.

Lucas shook his head. His dad had done the best he could, whereas Lucas had failed his father in so many ways. Right from being born when his dad was too young and changing the whole track of his life, through to Christmas Eve fourteen years ago when he should have stayed in, through to right now when he couldn't make it better — he'd failed every single time.

8

New Year's Eve, 2014

Jessica

'I'm fine.'

At the other end of the phone Michelle didn't sound convinced. 'Are you sure? It's not too late to get a flight up here.'

Jess hesitated. The idea of seeing her best friend was tempting, but a last minute flight would be expensive, and Michelle was ensconced at Sean's farm in the depths of the Scottish wilds. She had her own new husband, and no doubt Sean's family would be there in force. Jess wasn't sure she could cope with quite that much domestic bliss at the moment. 'I'll be fine. I'll come up and see you at half-term.'

She could almost hear the frown over the phone. Jess knew Michelle liked things dealt with properly. It must be breaking her up not being able to march around to Patrick's new girl-friend's flat and give the pair of them a piece of her mind. 'But you're not going to be on your own tonight? New Year's Eve can be weird. I don't want you getting all weepy and taking him back.'

Jess was glad her friend couldn't see her face. Would she take Patrick back? It didn't matter. She wasn't going to get the chance. All that was left was to put her brave face on, and carry on as best she could. 'I won't. I might see what Simon's doing.'

That seemed to satisfy Michelle. They talked for a few minutes more about Michelle's bump and about which of the eccentricities of Sean's family might turn out to be genetic, before Michelle rang off.

That left Jess with six hours to fill until 2014 was officially over. Her first instinct was to get in bed with a book and ignore the whole thing, but she knew it wouldn't work. She couldn't concentrate enough to read, and sleep hadn't been coming easily of late. She could do what she'd told Michelle and call Simon. No. She could do better than that. She could go round there. She knew her brother. He'd have people around for New Year. His clubbing days might be behind him, but he was a consummate host, and always had a houseful at New Year and on birthdays and holidays. The only time he didn't volunteer to play the host with the most was when their family was involved. Jess might find her mother a little judgemental, but Simon increasingly considered her beyond the pale.

On New Year's Eve he was bound to have friends around, and he'd be more than happy to include his little sister in the group. Jess pulled on her coat and then stopped. The flash of reflection in the hall mirror was not heartening. She still hadn't cried beyond the odd stray tear, so she'd escaped the classic pink blotchy heartbreak face, but nothing could disguise her grey pallor. Her hair was scraped back into a greasy, unloved ponytail. She didn't exactly look party ready.

Jess dragged herself to the bathroom and let the shower water run over her body. She wasn't entirely sure when the last time she'd taken a shower was, but there were lines of black grime under her fingernails, and her armpits had turned into a hairy sweaty fug. She didn't just need a shower. She needed industrial levels of scraping, tweezing and moisturizing. It was still early in the evening. She had time. It might be therapeutic. She could wash away the trauma of the last week, and transform herself into a new woman for the New Year.

Jess started with the simple stuff. Legs were shaved. Hair was washed and conditioned. Out of the shower, Jess trimmed and filed her nails before painting her toes and finger tips in deep purple. And then she stopped. The full length mirror showed her the reality. Tummy rounded with what, she believed, was known in her magazines as relationship weight. Dimples of cellulite on the backs of her thighs. Half a chin more than she was happy with. It was no use primping and preening. There was no way she could paint her tired married body, pushing thirty as it was, back to being twenty-one and ready for anything. She couldn't pluck out the memories of Patrick that were all around her, and inside her head. She couldn't wash the years of her life she'd wasted away. And they had been wasted. She'd been sensible. She'd taken things slow, and she'd ended up tossed aside anyway. Putting her face on and painting her nails wouldn't make her a new woman.

Instead of hunting for a party dress in the wardrobe, she pulled her balled up pyjamas from under the duvet and threw them on. It might be the start of a new year, but, whatever she did, she was still the same old Jess.

She dragged the duvet off the bed and carried it to the living room, before gathering her provisions together. Tissues. Leftover Christmas chocolate. Leftover Christmas alcohol. That was all she needed. There was no way she was venturing out there. 2014 had been horrible. There was no reason to start 2015 pretending it was going to be any different.

The door buzzer interrupted her wallowing. Jess glanced at the clock. Twenty to eight. She wasn't expecting anyone. A bubble of anticipation rose up from her belly. Patrick? It was New Year's Eve. It was the sort of night where people took stock and reflected on the mistakes of the past year. Maybe he was coming back to her. She jumped off the sofa and ran into the hallway, slamming her hand against the intercom button when she got there. 'Hello.'

'Hi.'

It wasn't Patrick. She squeezed her eyes tight shut against the tears that threatened to come but never quite fell. 'Who is it?'

The voice hesitated, and the intercom crackled with interference. ' . . . from Christmas. And Boxing Day.'

'Right.' Embarrassment replaced despair. The poor bloke she'd harangued into taking her to find Patrick. What on earth must he think of her? 'Come in. I guess.'

Jess raced into the bedroom. She might have already established that she couldn't primp herself into anything nearing an attractive state, but she could, at least, have clothes on.

New Year's Eve, 2014

Lucas

He shouldn't have come here. He ought to be with his dad, but his father seemed to want Lucas around even less since his latest hospitalisation, and he'd had no luck finding a place for them both to live. He could have gone home, but Trish and Charlie had invited a houseful of guests around and Lucas wasn't sure he was feeling up to an evening of making polite chit-chat and side-stepping personal questions. He needed to hide away and somehow he'd wondered if Jess might be doing the same.

He knocked on the door to the flat. 'One minute!'

He recognised the slightly panicked voice of somebody who hadn't been expecting guests. Of course, it was New Year's Eve. He'd pictured her home alone, but that was the girl he'd been imagining. Real-life Jess might have plans of her own. She might have guests. She might have let her husband move back in. That thought didn't sit well. Lucas promised himself that he wasn't here to try to rekindle some romance that had never really happened from years ago, but he was absolutely sure that she deserved to be with someone better than a cheating loser.

The door swung open. Jess waved a hand downwards towards her body.

'Sorry. I'm a bit scruffy. I wasn't really expecting anyone.'

Lucas glanced down. She was wearing clothes. He didn't really know about women's clothes. He lived in jeans, T-shirt and a hoodie. She was wearing jeans and a top. She looked fine to him. Better than fine. Much much better. He smiled. 'You look great.'

She was still leaning on the door frame looking at him.

'Right. Yeah. I just . . . ' Lucas's voice tailed off. What had he 'just'? 'I just wanted to see if you were okay.'

Jess's face broke slightly from the mask of anxiety he realised she normally wore, and the edges of her lips turned ever so slightly up. 'Yeah. Well no.' She shrugged. 'I don't know.'

'Right. Well, I'm free if you want somebody to hang out with.' He glanced towards the stairway, trying to sound nonchalant. 'Or I can go if you want.'

She inched the door all the way open. 'Come in.'

Lucas followed her into the living room, and waited while she hurriedly gathered a duvet from the floor. 'I don't normally have this in here. I was . . . sort of . . . '

'You were having a duvet day.'

She nodded. 'Well duvet night. I hate New Year's Eve.'

Lucas took a seat on the sofa and surveyed the bottles in various states of emptiness on the coffee table. He picked up a full beer and flicked the top off with the opener on his key ring. 'So do I. Last year Trish and Charlie made me go out on New Year's Eve. It was awful. Overpriced. Full of people who only go out once a year falling over after three shots.'

Jess sat down next to him. 'Last year I was on my honeymoon.'

Lucas closed his eyes. 'Sorry.'

'Me too. We went skiing. Flew out the day after Boxing Day for a week. I hate skiing.'

'Then why do it for your honeymoon?'

She pursed her lips. 'Patrick loves it. He said he'd teach me.'

'Didn't he?'

Jess shook her head. 'No. He went off on the big slopes, and left me in the beginner's class.'

Lucas frowned. It didn't sound like much of a honeymoon. 'Bet you had some rows about that.'

Jess frowned even deeper. 'No. We never argued.'

'Why not?' Lucas had never really had a long relationship, and he'd never had a mum and dad who lived together, so most of his understanding of long-term relationships was based on his house-mates, who were devoted to one another, and equally devoted to never losing a fight. 'Charlie and Trish row all the time.'

Jess took a deep slug of her drink. 'I don't like fighting. I hate it when people shout at me.'

Lucas grinned. 'I know what you mean. I had this . . . ' He paused. He'd almost said 'director.' 'There was a guy I worked for once who was always yelling at everyone. I used to feel sick every time he came anywhere near me. You never knew who was going to be the next person to get a rocket up their arse.'

'I know. And I didn't want Patrick to be upset. It was his honeymoon too.'

'So you never told him you were miserable?'

Jess pursed her lips. 'I wasn't miserable. I was happy that he was having a good time.' She paused a second. 'Anyway, what about you? Are you seeing anyone?'

Lucas shook his head. If he had been in a relationship he suspected that spending New Year's Eve alone with another woman would have been considered poor form. 'Free and single.'

'And how's your dad?'

'My dad?' Lucas didn't really talk about his dad. Even Trish and Charlie only knew that he had a dad who'd had some health problems. It wasn't something where he ever went into detail.

'He was in hospital?'

'He's home now.' That word — home.

Was his dad home? Was Morning Rise really the best place for him? 'I told you he lives in a care home sort of place? Well, he had a car accident, years ago, and it affected his brain. He can't really live on his own any more.'

'Oh my god. That's awful.'

Lucas paused. Was it awful? 'It's normal for me.'

'Tell me about it.'

Lucas took another gulp of beer. She was a stranger. This was a bubble of time. This sofa on the last night of the year. It was another bubble like that Christmas Eve kitchen all those years ago. Maybe . . . and so he started talking.

And it was easier than he expected. The words tumbled over one another rushing to be free. He told her about that night. Christmas Eve, fourteen years ago. He told her that he'd been out with a mate and got a call to say his dad was missing. He told her about the police officer who'd come to his hotel room on Christmas morning and patted him on the head and pointed out that his father was a grown man who would probably roll home of his own accord when he slept off whatever he'd had to drink the night before. Then he told her about the call from the hospital, and the feeling that everything in his world had fallen apart and would never quite fit back together again. He remembered the family his dad had driven straight into. He told her that they'd been forgiving, but that they were wrong. And once he'd started talking he felt like he might never stop. He might tell his girl from the kitchen everything.

New Year's Eve, 2014

Jessica

And Jess listened. She listened to the story of the two young girls whose lives had been affected forever by the accident. She listened to the stories of the care facilities that hadn't been able to cope with his dad. She listened to the stories from longer ago — the comic books and the days out. She listened to the stories from more recently — the increasingly bitter man who sometimes knew his son and sometimes didn't and sometimes, it appeared, pretended not to know out of little more than spite. 'It puts the things I've been crying over into perspective.'

At the other end of the sofa her guest frowned. 'Not at all. Being let down by someone you love is horrible.'

'That sounds like the voice of experience.'

He shook his head. 'No, but I let my dad down. That's what I always remember when he's yelling or throwing things or refusing to let me in. I should have been there, the night it happened. I let him down.'

Jess reached along the sofa and took his hand. It was meant to be a gesture of comfort. There was nothing comfortable about it. The jolt of heat that ran through her body was pure sex. At least she imagined it was. She wasn't sure she'd ever felt anything like it before.

She'd fancied Patrick. She'd known he was good-looking. She'd seen the way that other women looked at him. This was different. This wasn't about her finding someone attractive; it was about her suddenly feeling like a goddess when he touched her skin. She pulled her hand away. 'You were just a kid when he had the crash.'

He nodded.

'Then you weren't responsible. He was the adult. Not you.'

She watched her guest stare at his beer bottle for a moment.

'My childhood was kind of complicated. I . . . ' His voice cracked. She waited. 'I made quite a lot of money quite young. My dad wasn't used to being rich. It sort of went to his head a bit.' He shook his head. 'That's not fair. He was used to doing everything for me, and then when we had money maybe he felt like he wasn't needed? Or maybe he didn't know how to cope? He drank. A lot. Too much. He was drunk when he crashed the car. I knew what he was like.' She watched him screw his eyes tight shut. 'I knew what he was like and I went out anyway. I thought it was more important for me to go out with my mate and have a laugh than stay in with him.' He opened his eyes and looked straight at Jess. 'It was my fault.'

Jess recognised the child the man in front of her used to be. She'd had kids like that in her class. Kids from tough households. Kids who'd learnt to fend for themselves. Kids who'd grown up looking out for younger brothers and sisters, or for the parents who were supposed to look after them. Kids who wore a permanent mask of 'everything's all right.' Some of those kids got good at wearing that mask. Some never did. 'What were you doing?'

'What?'

'The night he had the accident, what were you doing?'

He stared at the floor for a second. 'Just went out with a mate. Stupid teenage boy stuff.'

'Right.' Jess could see that he didn't

want to talk about it, and she didn't think she knew him well enough to force the issue. She needed a change of subject. 'So, what do you do now?'

'How do you mean?'

'Like for work and that.'

He shrugged. 'Bits and bobs.'

'Okay.' So he did something dodgy that he didn't want to talk about. That didn't fit with the image in Jess's head. 'I'm a teacher.'

'What age?'

'Primary.' Jess sighed. She'd messed up, hadn't she? He'd been baring his soul, but somehow she'd said the wrong thing, and now he'd clammed up again. 'Another drink?'

She gestured towards the stack of booze, and watched as he flicked open another beer. His brow furrowed as he took an extended slug, before turning towards her. 'Look. I'm sorry. I've not been completely honest with you.'

Jess's stomach clenched. Of course he hadn't been honest. People weren't, were they? Patrick hadn't been. Why would this guy be any different?

'My name isn't Alan.'

Jess nodded. She sort of knew that already.

'It's Lucas.' He was staring at her full in the face. 'I'm Lucas.'

New Year's Eve, 2014

Lucas

He looked into her face, waiting for a flicker of recognition. There was none. He took a deep breath. He wasn't entirely sure what he was doing, but he wasn't entirely sure why he'd come to this virtual stranger's home on New Year's Eve, and he wasn't entirely sure why he'd been unable to stop thinking about her since she'd turned up at his house on Christmas Day, but he was here, and he was ever so slightly drunk, and so he'd decided that, for once, he would turn off his brain and let his mouth lead the way. 'My real name is Lucas Woods.'

This time there was a flicker. He took

a deep breath. 'I don't really have a job at the moment, because of caring for my dad, and because I don't need the money, so I volunteer at an advice centre and on an addiction helpline.' He wasn't looking at her face now. If he saw her reaction that might be enough to make him stop. 'And I don't need the money because — '

'You're the *Miracle at the North Pole* kid!'

Lucas nodded.

Jess's jaw hung open. 'I thought you'd gone off the rails or something.'

It was what everyone thought. His dad's accident had made it into the papers, but with a couple of key details all the wrong way around. They'd picked up that the police were involved and that the car was hired on Lucas's account, and then Lucas had disappeared from public view, having been one of the best known actors on the planet for the previous five years. Once you added in the received wisdom that child stars always ended up losing the plot, it had been pretty easy for people to put two and two together and make something a long way north of four. 'I didn't go off the rails.'

'But your dad did?'

Lucas nodded. 'He was only in his twenties when I made my first movie, and he'd never had money before. Not like that anyway.'

'I can't believe you're a film star.'

'Was a film star. In the past.'

'Why did you stop?' She was frowning. 'Was it because of your dad?'

Lucas paused. Why had he stopped? He'd always told himself he stopped because of his dad. He'd been supposed to start filming on a weird cowboys and robots sci-fi western thing that January, a few weeks after the accident, but he'd pulled out. Why had he never gone back? Honesty, he'd decided was his watchword for the night. 'It was too much, everybody knowing who I was, everybody thinking they had a part of me.'

'So you liked the actual acting?'

He didn't know how to answer. In his

head acting was all to do with the movie business, and that was all to do with fame and fakery, which he'd grown to detest. He thought back to drama club, before that first audition, back when he was playing second spear carrier in the background. 'It was okay.'

He paused. It wasn't the actual acting that he loved. 'I loved being part of a company. Even on the big movies. I liked working with all the other actors and the crew.' Lucas smiled. 'I wasn't that good though.'

Jess shrugged. 'You seemed to do okay.'

Lucas shook his head. 'I was lucky. For *Miracle* I just had to look innocent and make a few cute quips. And looking innocent was easy because I didn't have a clue what was going on. Nowt I did after that was any good though.'

He watched Jess's face change.

'What?'

She took a slug of her drink. 'Well I don't want to be rude, but most of what you did after that was awful.'

'Thanks.'

'No. I mean the films were awful. You were fine in them, but they were bad bad movies.'

'I didn't have you down as a film buff.'

Jess smiled. 'I'm younger than any of my brothers by like fifteen years which meant I had to entertain myself a lot, and so I persuaded my mum and dad to get me a TV and a VHS for my bedroom. If you could get it from the local library I've seen it.'

Lucas winced. 'Then I should probably be apologising to you.'

Jess shook her head. '*Miracle at the North Pole* is one of my favourite films. I cry at the end every time.'

Lucas hesitated. Honesty, he reminded himself. 'I've never seen it.'

'What?' Jess's eyes widened. 'Everyone's seen it.'

Lucas shook his head. 'I was too young to stay up for the premiere, so I walked down the red carpet and then got back in the car in an alley behind the cinema. So I didn't see it then, and paying to go see it at a regular screening seemed weird, so I never did.' He stopped. He thought he might be all talked out. He told her all the things he usually kept locked away, and now he was . . . what? Lighter? Definitely. Happier? He wasn't sure. He was spent though. He knew that. He took a long gulp from his drink. 'I'm going on about me. How are you?'

Jess shrugged. 'Single. Apparently.'

'I'm sorry.'

She laughed. 'You're the only one that is. Everyone else either thinks I was a lousy wife because I couldn't even keep hold of him a year, or tells me I'm better off without him.'

'Well I agree with the better off without him people, obviously. But I'm sorry you're sad.'

New Year's Eve, 2014

Jessica

He was sorry she was sad, and she definitely was sad. She'd been sad all week. Really she'd been sad since September when she'd found out about Patrick's affair with Cora, and realised that her whole idea of what her own life was like was a fantasy. She blinked her eyes tight shut to block out the world for a second. Being sad wasn't getting her anywhere, and when she thought about it, Jess realised, the harsh ball of wretchedness in her guts wasn't quite there anymore. Not right at this moment at least. Right this second what she was feeling wasn't sadness. It was something else entirely.

Lucas was sitting next to her on the sofa, body twisted towards her, his face full of concern. She raised her head and looked back into his bright green eyes. She hadn't really looked at his face properly before. She'd been preoccupied with Patrick and the marriage-wrecking harlot. It was a good face, a really good face. Patrick was always perfectly put together, clean-shaven, groomed — Jess had a suspicion that he tweezed his eyebrows. Lucas was a man who didn't bother with any such vanities. His chin was lined with stubble, and his brown hair was functionally short — the sort of hair that could be washed and then safely ignored. Michelle had always called Patrick a 'pretty boy.' Lucas wasn't pretty, and he definitely wasn't a boy.

'Are you okay?'

'What?' Jess shifted back in her seat. She hadn't been leaning towards him, had she?

'You were looking at me funny.'

'Sorry.' Jess stopped. Was she sorry? She'd spent a lot of time recently being sorry. She'd said sorry to her parents for running out on Christmas dinner. She'd said sorry to Cora for crashing her Christmas Day. She'd said sorry to Lucas for using him as a chauffeur service. She even thought she might have said sorry to Patrick. She was sick of being sorry. She was sick of acting like everything she'd done was wrong. And she was sick of being sensible. She'd been sensible all her life, and where had it got her? She pulled her glass to her lips. It was empty. That didn't seem right. She'd planned to keep filling it up until the bottles of random alcohol were all gone. She didn't think it ought to be empty yet at all. She refocused on Lucas and fought her way back to her train of thought. That was it. Sorry. Being sorry. Not being sorry. Not apologising for every little thing. 'I'm not sorry.'

He frowned. 'Okay. What are you not sorry for?'

'For snogging you.'

The frown deepened, but a hint of a smile tugged at the edges of his lips. 'You haven't snogged me.'

Jess thought through the conversation. He was right. She hadn't snogged him. That was embarrassing. 'Sorry. I didn't mean . . . I . . . ' Jess listened to her own voice, doing what it always did. Apologising. Avoiding awkwardness. Not saying what she wanted. It was the last night of the year. It was a man she could simply choose never to see again.

Why not go for it for once? Why not see what it would be like to be Cora or Victoria or any one of those perfect, confident women who got the things they desired? She didn't let herself hesitate. Hesitation would leave time for reflection and reflection would lead the way to thinking about risks and consequences. She didn't want to do any of that. She leant towards him, bringing her hand to his cheek as she pressed her lips to his.

New Year's Eve, 2014

Lucas

He hadn't expected her to kiss him. He'd hoped. He couldn't kid himself that he hadn't hoped. He'd told himself he was going to see her because he was avoiding the party at home, or because he was at a loose end, or because he was worried about her, but really he'd come to see her because he was hoping that whatever had been there in that kitchen fourteen years ago would still be there now. He'd hoped that whatever it was that had come over him when he'd seen her standing on the doorstep on Christmas Day might have come over her as well. He'd thought it was foolish to hope; he'd pretended that he wasn't hoping at all, but hope was never quite that easily put down.

She pulled away from his lips. 'Sorry.'

'What?'

'Sorry. That was . . . you probably don't . . . ' She stared for a second at the bottle and glasses on the table. 'I should clear these . . . ' She stood and started gathering debris into her arms.

'Wait.' Lucas had messed this up, but for once in his life he knew exactly how he'd messed up. He'd forgotten that he was supposed to be being honest. He'd started thinking about the kiss, and wondering what it meant. He'd forgotten to stop worrying and kiss the damn girl back. 'Wait.'

He stood up and lifted the bottles out of her hand. She pursed her lips slightly. 'What are you doing?'

'What I should have done two hours ago.' Lucas placed one hand on her waist and the other to the side of her face, before lowering his lips to meet hers. She responded immediately, snaking her arms around his neck and pulling him towards her. This felt honest.

He let her lead, sliding her hands under his T-shirt and peeling the fabric away from his skin. He followed her to the bedroom, watching as she slipped her own top over her head, before finding his belt with her fingers and pulling and fumbling to release him. He grinned as she swore to herself under her breath as she tipped out the contents of her bedside drawer hunting for a condom, and then he took her beneath him and all around him and let her soothe him and stop him thinking about anything at all beyond the scent, and touch, and taste of the very second he was living in.

9

New Year's Day, 2015

Jessica

'Happy New Year.'

Jess swallowed hard. Someone seemed to have stuffed her mouth with sand while she was asleep. She forced an eye open, and lifted her head from the pillow. The voice was lying next to her in bed. It smiled. 'Happy New Year.'

'What time is it?'

'Nearly ten.'

Jess shook her head. 'Don't believe you. Still the middle of the night.'

She closed her eyes for a second. She was in bed with Lucas. She hadn't woken up in her own bed with anyone who wasn't Patrick for years. There'd been men, during her and Patrick's 'off' periods, but none that had been serious enough to stay the night for a very long time. It ought to feel awkward. It didn't. Being here with him felt like the most natural thing she could imagine. She opened her eyes again. 'Happy New Year to you too.'

The daylight coming in through the curtains was too much for Jess's drink-addled retinas. She closed her eyes. Flashes of last night whipped through her mind. The scent of his skin as she buried her face in the crook of his neck. The roughness of his stubble against her cheek. The warmth of his body beside her as she drifted into sleep. And then other things. Snippets of conversation. Oh god. Jess pulled the duvet up to cover her reddening cheeks.

'What's up?' He gently tugged the covers away from her face.

'I'm sorry.'

'What for?'

'I said all your films were shite. I'm so sorry.' Jess was mortified. She could blame the alcohol. She could blame a stressful week, but it was no excuse. 'I'd never normally say that.'

She forced herself to look at his face. He was grinning. 'You were honest. No need to apologise for that.'

'But I'm so sorry.'

'You said. And it's fine.' Lucas turned over and shifted down the bed so he was lying on his side facing her. 'So do you have any plans today?'

Jess shook her head. New Year's Day had always seemed like a peculiarly pointless bank holiday. It was a day entirely set aside for sleeping off hangovers and throwing away Christmas food that was turning manky. 'What about you?'

'Well I need to go see my dad later, but I could go this evening, if you wanted to do . . . something?'

She nodded.

'Like a date sort of something?' he added.

Jess nodded again. Why shouldn't she go on a date? Why shouldn't she have her fresh start?

'Okay. I don't know about you but I need something to eat.'

Jess realised that that could be a problem. 'I haven't been to the shop since ... well, you know. I'd basically got down to leftover booze and Quality Street.'

And she was pretty sure they'd cleared the leftover booze already.

Lucas grinned. 'All right then. I guess we'll start by finding somewhere for breakfast. What do you reckon? Coffee shop and croissants? Or full English?'

Jess's hangover answered before her budding resolution to lose weight had a chance to intervene. 'Bacon. Need bacon.'

So an hour later they were snuggled into a booth in a less than stylish pub chomping their way through bacon, eggs, sausage, beans, mushrooms, tomatoes and toast. They'd established that brown sauce was very wrong, and agreed to disagree about ketchup at breakfast time. And Jess had discovered that she was hungry. Ravenous. It was her first proper meal in a week, since she abandoned Christmas dinner and set off to walk across the city. And now she was out with her new man. Everything had worked out. Really, when she thought about it, it was for the best that she'd found out about Patrick's affair, because that's what had brought her here.

'Jess!'

Lucas's voice brought her back to the table. 'Sorry. What?'

'Nothing. You were miles away.'

She smiled. 'Sorry. I was just thinking about Patrick.'

His eyes narrowed slightly.

'Not like that. Just that it's all worked out. I know my brother and Michelle, my friend, they were expecting me to fall apart but I didn't. I got through it and now we're here.'

Lucas didn't answer straight away. 'You don't have to be okay, you know.'

'But I'm fine.'

'Okay. But it was only a week ago. This . . . ' he waved his fork to gesture the space between the two of them. 'We can take this slow, if that's what you want.'

Jess shook her head. 'I told you. I'm fine.'

'All right. So what else do you want to do?'

She didn't know. She was used to Patrick having an idea or a plan. She was used to going skiing because he wanted to go skiing. She was used to entertaining herself on her own in her room, because her brothers were too big to be interested in her. She was used to Michelle organising her and giving advice. 'I don't know. What do you want to do?'

Lucas leant back. 'Let's be tourists.'

'What do you mean?'

'Let's go to one of the parks, or Harrods, or Madame Tussauds, or the zoo.'

'Harrods on a Bank Holiday during the sale?'

'No. Fair point. You know what I mean though. How long have you lived in London?'

'Er . . . we . . . I moved here after Uni, so nine years.'

'Okay. I've been here about five. And how often do either of us actually go out and do tourist stuff?'

She shook her head. 'Never?'

'Well then.'

So they walked the length of Regent's Park, bundled up in coats, scarves and gloves against the January chill. Jess felt like all the big, serious talk had been spent last night, so they talked about little things. It was silly inconsequential chatter, but when they reached the gates of London Zoo, Jess found she didn't want to go in. 'I'm happy just walking, if that's okay.'

Lucas nodded. 'That's fine.'

'I'd forgotten how much I like Christmas.'

'It's not really Christmas anymore.'

'Course it is. It's Christmas until I have to go back to school, thank you very much.'

'Tell me what you like about it.' She felt his fingers rub against hers as he spoke, and she wrapped her hand around his.

'Well, it's romantic.'

'You still think that?'

She nodded. 'I got married at Christmas for a reason.' Another memory stirred. 'I had my first kiss at Christmas as well.' Had she told him that already? 'It was at this stupid party of some friend of my mum's.'

Her arm pulled backwards, and she realised Lucas had stopped walking. She turned around. 'What's up?'

'There's something else I should have told you last night.'

The knot in her stomach reappeared. Maybe it had never really gone away. 'What?'

'It's not a bad thing. I don't think. It's romantic.'

'Just tell me.'

He was gazing down at the floor. 'We've actually met before.'

'On Christmas Day?'

'No. *Before* before. Years ago.' He lifted her face and stared straight at her. Those bright green eyes.

'No.'

169

'Jess!'

'No.' It didn't make sense. He couldn't be. Of course he could be. She hadn't connected the Alans because she'd known, this time around at least, that that wasn't his real name. 'I asked you. I asked you if we knew each other.'

'I know.' He was still gripping her hand. 'I just . . . I don't really talk about my past, and you were upset, and there was never a good moment.'

'Last night? The whole of last night there was no good moment?'

She pulled her hand away from his. There was too much going on inside her head to process. She couldn't make sense of it all. Patrick lied. She'd accepted that, and she'd decided that she was moving on, and Lucas was different. That's what she'd thought. Lucas was going to be different. Lucas wasn't going to make her feel out of control, and like she was constantly swallowing back this wave of darkness that threatened to overwhelm her. One thought crystallised in front of her. 'You lied.'

170

'I'm sorry. I didn't mean to.'

It didn't matter. 'You lied. You lied to me last night. And you lied to me back then.'

'No!'

'You did. You told me your name was Alan. That was pretty much all you told me about yourself and it was a lie.' And that was it, wasn't it? Men lied to her. 'That was where it all started . . . '

'What?'

She was right. She could see it all now. 'That was where it all started. You were the first. I liked you. I thought you liked me. But you lied and then you just . . . you went away.'

'I'm sorry.'

Jess shook her head. They were always sorry. And then Jess was sorry. Everyone was sorry. Patrick had been sorry, at least the first time. Sorry didn't mean anything. 'I want you to go.'

'What? No. We can sort this out.'

'No. I want you to go.' She risked a glance at his face. He looked defeated.

She repeated her point. 'I want you to go.'

He stood a few feet away for a few seconds before he nodded.

'And I never want to see you again.'

Jess waited until his back was receding into the distance before she walked the few yards to the nearest bench and sat down. At least she'd done better this time. With Patrick she'd listened to his explanations and apologies and she'd taken him back. At least she'd learnt. This time she'd been sensible. Lucas was a worse sort of liar. He was the sort who made you believe he was telling the truth. And then, finally, she started to cry.

2015

10

23rd December, 2015

Jessica

'I can't believe you're moving two days before Christmas.' Michelle was sitting on the floor in Jess's now bare living room, bouncing Jess's nine-month old goddaughter, Izzy, in her arms.

Jess looked around the bare room. The sale wasn't scheduled to complete until January 2nd, but she hadn't wanted to wait any longer. An extra fortnight's rent in her new apartment was more than she could afford but worth it in the circumstances. 'I don't want another Christmas in this flat.'

Michelle cuddled her baby girl. 'So what next?'

'Well new flat obviously. Once this is

sold Patrick will get his half of the equity.'

'I can't believe you're giving him half.'

Jess shot her best friend a look. 'His parents helped with the deposit.'

'And then he promptly lost his job and spent the rest of your marriage shagging around.'

It was true, but there was no point getting wound up about it now. 'It was the easiest way to get it over with. This way the divorce will be done by the end of next month.'

'I know.' Michelle pulled a face at her little girl. 'But that wasn't what I meant.'

'What then?'

'What's next romantically?'

Jess shook her head. 'You've changed.'

'What do you mean?'

'What happened to the woman who said romance was just a posh word for deceit?'

Michelle's husband appeared in the doorway. 'She's a convert.'

Michelle shook her head. 'I am not,

but I think it would do Jess good to get out there again.'

Sean pulled a face. 'She doesn't need to put herself out there. She's got the reappearing Christmas Kiss guy.'

Jess knew Sean was unlikely to let this one drop, but there was really nothing to talk about. 'I think that was over before it began.'

Sean frowned. 'No chance. Two meetings. Years apart. Both at Christmas. That sounds meant to be to me.'

Michelle set Izzy down on the floor and struggled to her feet. The little girl set off, shuffling on her bottom towards Daddy. 'Don't be ridiculous. I'm not saying she should fall in love straight away, just that it might be good for her to get out and meet new people. The Christmas guy was a rebound thing. That never works.'

Jess nodded.

Sean crouched down to pick up his little girl. 'But that's my point. You can't choose when you fall in love. Love is just love. There's no right time or right way of finding it.'

'But he lied about who he was.'

'I know.' Sean shuffled to let Izzy get settled against his chest. 'But everybody lies, sometimes. It depends why he lied.'

'No!'

Jess listened to their argument. Michelle was right. She'd thrown caution to the wind with Lucas a year ago and, of course, it had been a mistake. The bickering rumbled on around her. She coughed loudly. 'I'm still in the room.'

Her friends exchanged a glance. 'Sorry.'

Sean nodded. 'Ignore us. I'm a hopeless romantic and she's got no soul.'

'Oh, I know.'

'But, have you thought about getting in touch with him?'

Jess didn't answer. Of course she'd thought about it. She'd almost done it a hundred times, but the realistic conclusion was that she'd missed her chance. Maybe she could have called him that very first day and said she'd overreacted. Maybe she could have explained that she was still upset about Patrick, and she hadn't meant to take it out on him. She could have called him and said sorry, but what was the point? There was no point trying, no point pretending that it had been anything more than a fling. And so that first day had turned into a second day, and then a week, and a month and she'd had to accept that he wasn't going to call her, and she'd missed the moment to call him. It was probably for the best, when she'd had so much else to think about — filling divorce forms in, selling her flat, dividing up her and Patrick's things. 'Maybe we could concentrate on the moving?'

Sean sighed. 'Okay. All the boxes are in the van. Apart from . . . '

'From what?'

He gestured towards the bedroom door. 'There's one marked *Patrick*. I wasn't sure what you wanted to do with it.'

Jess hesitated. It wasn't anything important. Patrick had sent his father to collect his clothes and computer in January, and she'd made Simon drop off the few bits of furniture she couldn't bear to keep using. What was left was tat really, stuff that she'd found over the year and couldn't quite bring herself to throw away. 'I guess I'll take it to him.'

Michelle frowned but didn't object. Jess didn't need her to. She was well aware that her best friend would have cheerfully dowsed Patrick's stuff in petrol and chucked in a flame. There'd been moments over the last twelve months when Jess would have lent her the lighter.

Sean cleared his throat. 'We could take it, if you want.'

Jess shook her head. 'You've done loads to help already. I'll take the box to Patrick's and meet you at the new place.'

Sean strapped Izzy into the car seat in the van, and Jess watched as her possessions drove away. She stuffed the box of Patrick's things into the boot of her own car and set off across London.

She found a parking space around the corner from the florist shop she'd visited a year before and pulled in. The street was busy with last minute Christmas shoppers, and she struggled through the crowd with the taped up box. She rang the buzzer for 17a and waited.

23rd December, 2015

Lucas

Lucas pulled into the car park at Morning Rise. He'd promised himself he wouldn't still be coming here. He'd promised himself that this was going to be the year when he took responsibility properly, and he'd tried. He'd really tried. He'd found a ground floor flat with a secure garden. He'd talked to social workers and advisers from the local carers' helpline and to consultants and addiction specialists. He'd done it. He'd moved his dad out of the home and in with him. And he'd lasted seven weeks.

Seven weeks.

Seven weeks before he found himself fighting with his dad in the hallway, because he'd picked up Lucas's car keys and made a dash for freedom. Seven weeks from absolutely believing that what he was doing was for the best, to physically restraining the man who raised him, while his dad struggled and kicked and spat. Seven weeks to realise that wanting to care for his dad wasn't the same as being able to.

So now his dad was back here, and Lucas was back to driving across the capital every day to visit. Only now he was doing it from an empty flat. He got to the room, knocked, and pushed the door open. There were Christmas decorations up inside his father's room, which was a first. Normally he had a fit of temper when decorations were mentioned, but this year he'd been part of the occupational therapy group making streamers and had consented to a string across the ceiling. 'How are you today?'

The older man looked up from his chair by the window. 'Lukey!'

Lucas smiled. 'Hi Dad.'

'I was watching a squirrel.' He gestured out towards the garden. 'It's gone now. Do you remember the squirrels in Roundhay Park, Lukey?'

Lucas nodded. He realised now that his dad took him to the park so often because he could get a bus straight there and it was free once they arrived, but at the time the wide green space had been his personal playground. 'Are you looking forward to Christmas?'

'Yeah.' His dad went back to staring out of the window. 'It were in Roundhay Park that your mum told me she was pregnant.'

Lucas didn't reply. His dad never talked about his mother. It wasn't a secret exactly. Lucas had met his mum; he knew who she was. She'd been fourteen when she had Lucas, and she was just too young to cope. His dad had never taught him to be angry or bitter about that, and he knew that his mum was married now with kids still in primary school. She sent him cards at Christmas and birthdays, but she was never talked about.

'She were so scared, but I wasn't. Everyone said it wasn't fair on you, trying to bring you up when I was just a kid, but you were my son. I was going to make sure you had the most incredible life. I wanted you to have everything. I wanted you to be able to do anything you wanted.' His dad didn't look at him. 'Did I do all right?'

Lucas swallowed hard. 'You did brilliantly.'

'Good. That's all you want when you're a dad. You want your kids to be happy.' His dad turned back towards him and scanned across the room. 'There was a thing about your film in the paper. Mrs Julia showed me it.'

The manager, Julia, was one of the few people who knew Lucas's full story. 'It's twenty years since it came out. They're re-releasing it.'

'Can we go Lukey?'

Lucas had actually been invited to a 'premiere' for the re-release in Leicester Square, but he'd politely declined, and it would be too much for his dad anyway. 'Maybe next week. Or we could get the DVD?'

His dad fell silent and then looked up, as if he'd forgotten Lucas was there for a moment. 'Have you brought my lunch?'

'You've had lunch. It's nearly dinner time.'

His dad nodded but didn't respond.

11

23rd December, 2015

Jessica

Jess had never thought she'd be back here again. She pressed the buzzer and waited. A woman's voice crackled over the intercom. 'Yes?'

'I've got a delivery.' Jess wasn't sure if that was the best thing to say, but she was aware that if she explained who she was the beautiful Victoria might not deign to open the door. As it was, she was buzzed in without another word.

Jess dragged the box up the stairs, and rapped on the door to 17a. She could hear slow footsteps from inside.

'Just a minute!'

Eventually the door swung open. Jess took a moment to process the evidence of her eyes. Victoria was still beautiful. She still had the same buzz cut hair on top of huge dark brown eyes and perfect cheekbones. She was radiant. You might say glowing, because she was also pregnant. It was hard to tell exactly under the voluminous maternity top she was wearing, but from what Jess could see, Victoria was very very pregnant indeed.

'So he's sent you?

'What?'

'He's sent you to get his things. Typical.'

Jess opened her mouth and closed it again. She wasn't getting his things. She was bringing his things. 'No. I don't understand.'

'Jessie!'

The voice behind her made her spin around. Patrick. Standing on the stairs holding his key.

Victoria snorted. 'So you both came. Awesome.'

'What are you doing here Jessie?' She decided to focus on Patrick's question, because at least it was one she could answer.

'I'm moving house. I found some of your things. I thought you might need them.'

'What things?'

In the doorway, Victoria opened her mouth and closed it again before she spoke. 'Is this some kind of joke?'

Jess shook her head.

'But Patrick doesn't live here. He left. He went back to . . . ' Victoria held a finger out pointing, accusingly, straight at Jess.

'What?' Jess turned to her ex.

He shrugged. 'Well it wasn't working out and . . . '

His words washed over her as the shock sunk in. Patrick wasn't with Victoria any more. That shouldn't be surprising. Long-term didn't seem to be one of his favoured things, but all year Jess had been picturing the two of them together, snuggled up in cosmopolitan domestic bliss, drinking overpriced wine and laughing at stories of Patrick's provincial-minded ex-wife. Of course that wasn't what he was doing. Patrick was built to want things, she realised. Once he had them, he inevitably wanted something else.

Victoria leaned against the door frame. 'So he didn't come back to you?'

Jess shook her head. She wasn't sure what the other woman was going to do. What if the shock sent her into labour right here? Jess really wasn't certain what the socially acceptable thing to do would be in those sort of circumstances.

Victoria's face froze for a second, and then cracked, not into the tears Jess might have expected, but into a huge, uncontrollable laugh. When she did her whole face crumpled into something far less perfect. Less beautiful, much prettier.

'Are you okay?'

'I'm fine.' Victoria nodded, and something inside Jess broke a little. That wasn't right. She shouldn't be fine. She was pregnant. She should have a partner she could rely on.

Patrick cleared his throat. 'So if I could just get my things?'

The feeling in Jess's gut exploded out of control. It wasn't a nice feeling. It wasn't a quiet feeling. It was the sort of feeling that might make somebody cause a scene. 'How could you?'

She screamed the words at Patrick, still skulking two steps below her.

'How could you? Who have you run off with this time? You absolute sleaze.'

Patrick held up his hands. 'Come on, Jess. What makes you think there's someone else? Maybe I did leave her for you.'

Had he? She paused but only for a second. 'Don't be ridiculous. You don't care about me, or her, or Cora or whoever you've shacked up with this time. You're just a . . . '

She ran out of steam. There weren't any words for what he was.

Victoria leaned forward. 'You said sleaze before.'

'Yes!' Jess could hear that she was yelling. She wasn't a person who yelled. She wasn't a person who acted on impulse. She wasn't a person who threw things either. She bent down and opened the box of his things. 'I brought your stuff back.'

One by one she hurled the contents of the box down the steps to where her ex-husband was cowering. A possibly broken charger for his electric razor whipped past his ear. A set of Russian dolls with faces like American presidents clapped him square in the chest. A box of cufflinks bounced off his shoe.

'Can I chuck something?'

Jess turned towards her former rival. 'Help yourself.'

'This is ridiculous. If you two can't act like adults, I don't have to stand here and take it.'

And the anger subsided as quickly as it had arrived, and Jess found herself laughing. Patrick's prettiness looked like vanity. His assertiveness was just high-handedness. All those years when she'd thought she was dragging her feet, and he was ready to commit, were an illusion. He'd wanted her precisely because she was just out of reach. Once they were married it was only a matter of time before things fell apart. Whatever it was that he'd held over her, even during a year of absence, was gone. The two women watched him stalk away down the stairs.

'Wow.'

'What?'

'Patrick told me you were a quiet little thing.'

Jess smiled. 'Well isn't it always the quiet ones you have to watch?'

'I am sorry.'

'Did you know he was married?'

Victoria shook her head. 'Not at first. And then he told me . . . ' Her voice tailed off. 'He told me you didn't understand him.' She closed her eyes as she uttered the cliché.

'And you believed him?'

'I guess I wanted to. I am sorry though.'

Jess waited for a new wave of anger, but it didn't come.

Victoria looked her up and down.

'You look different from a year ago.'

'How?'

'I don't know. Brighter somehow.'

'Thanks.' She jumped down a couple of steps and picked up the cufflinks and the Russian dolls, and chucked them back in the box. 'I guess he didn't want these.'

Victoria shook her head. 'I can get one of the neighbours to put it out by the bins if you want.'

It was a curiously unceremonious ending for a marriage, but somehow it felt right. 'Will you be okay?'

'I'll be fine. If you'd said a year ago that I'd be about to become a single mum, I'd have run a mile, but actually it's all good.' She rested a hand on top of her expansive belly. 'Really good. What about you?'

Jess paused. What about her? It had been a horrible year. She'd reached a point of acceptance. She wasn't intoxicating like Cora or Victoria. She wasn't the girl destined to get the guy, but when she'd seen Victoria's belly, and thought of her ex starting a whole new family, the pang hadn't hurt like she'd expected it to. 'I'm okay.'

She turned away to start down the stairs.

'Jessica!'

She stopped.

'I really am sorry, about . . . '

Jess shook her head. 'It's fine. It's over.'

The other woman smiled. 'So no regrets?'

Jess nodded in agreement. No regrets. 'Actually one thing. Not a regret. A parting gift, if you like.'

'What?'

'I've sold our flat. Patrick's getting half the money. Just so you know.'

Victoria frowned.

'For when he tells you he can't afford to pay child support.'

The other woman nodded. 'Thank you.'

She walked down the stairs, and along the crowded street. She'd parked, she realised now, in the same place that Lucas had stopped a year ago, when they'd driven around the back streets looking for her car. No regrets, she'd said, but that wasn't quite true. No regrets over Patrick maybe, but Patrick wasn't the person on her mind. Christmas ought to remind her of her December wedding, but it didn't. The fairy lights, the Christmas tunes, the mince pies all sent her back to that kitchen fifteen years ago. They sent her back to that sofa on New Year's Eve twelve months ago. Being cautious about love was the sensible choice. There was no reason to think that Lucas had even given her a second thought. Jess told herself to stop, but every time she thought about Lucas a tiny nugget of hope crept into her heart. She had to stop. Hope wasn't her friend. Hope was just the thing that came before disappointment.

Christmas Eve, 2015

Lucas

What his dad wanted him to do was be happy. That was all. He wanted Lucas to have an incredible life. Lucas wasn't sure that hiding away in his flat, rarely even telling anyone his real name, could be considered an incredible life. He wasn't sure that what he was about to do was the best first step to remedying that, but at least he was trying. He gripped the box tightly in one hand and rang the doorbell.

'Fake Alan!' Charlie flung herself through the door and hugged him vigorously. 'We thought you'd done a runner. Or the mafia finally caught up with you or something. That's it, isn't it? You're hiding from the mafia.'

He shook his head. 'Can I come in?'

'Course you can come in. Don't you still have a key?'

He followed his former housemate into the lounge.

'Look who I found.'

He was greeted with similar enthusiasm by Trish.

'Cora not around?'

Trish grinned. 'Cora has moved in with lovely Liam.'

That was a shame. Well, obviously it was good, for Cora, but Lucas had planned to do this once for the whole group. Never mind. In for a penny and all that.

The two women squashed onto the sofa on either side of their guest. 'So what brings you here?'

He took a deep breath. 'I hoped you might fancy a Christmas movie night?'

Charlie nodded. 'Always.' She grabbed the box from his hand. 'So what's the movie?'

He watched her scan the DVD case. '*Miracle at the North Pole*. Good choice.'

'Didn't we have that last year?'

'No.' Charlie narrowed her eyes. 'Fake Alan didn't want to watch it last year.' Her face suddenly broke into a smile. 'Pay up.'

'What?' Trish was looking blank.

'I think you owe me twenty quid.'

'What are you two talking about?'

Charlie turned the DVD box around and tapped her fingertip against the picture of Lucas's ten year-old face on the cover. 'Anything you want to tell us?'

Lucas leaned back. 'You already know?'

She raised an eyebrow. 'Know what?'

He took a deep breath. He'd come here to tell his closest friends the truth. And being a real friend, Charlie was going to make him go through with it. 'You already know that I'm Lucas Woods. I'm the kid in that film.'

Trish leapt off the sofa. 'No!' She jabbed him in the chest. 'You take that back. I'm not having her win a bet that's stood for the last six years. You tell her you're an undercover detective and you do it right now.'

Lucas laughed. 'Sorry. I can't believe you already knew.'

Charlie leaned her head against his shoulder. 'I didn't *know* know. I suspected.'

'But you never guessed that? And you guessed everything.'

She swallowed and glanced at her girlfriend. 'I didn't guess that because I thought it might be true. I figured it was up to you to tell us.' She grinned.

'And now you did, and she owes me twenty quid.'

Trish sat back down. 'Okay. Okay. She wasn't as restrained as she's making out though. Last Christmas she wanted to do an intervention on you.'

'Why?'

'She saw a documentary about them.'

Charlie nodded enthusiastically. 'They do them for alcoholics and that to help them get over denial. They look awesome.'

Lucas shook his head and tried to take it all in. 'When did you work it out?'

'About twenty minutes after you came to look at the room. I love Christmas movies. You know I love Christmas movies. I pretty much recognised you before you'd had chance to get your coat off.'

'So does everyone know who I am?'

His friends shook their heads.

'Don't think so,' Trish reassured him. 'I mean some of them might have thought that you look like that guy from that film, but you say you're called Alan and people go along with it. It's a bit different if you're living with someone.'

'So what else haven't you told us?'

'What do you mean?'

Charlie held up the DVD box. 'Well this was twenty years ago. I know you made a couple more films after this, and then you turned up here. Fill in the gaps a bit?'

'I wouldn't know where to start.'

Trish folded her arms. 'The beginning.'

And so Lucas talked. He told them the story of his dad's accident. And then he told them about the visit to his dad's previous care home in Leeds when his father had persuaded an agency gardener to bring him in a bottle of whisky. Lucas relived the terror of going into his father's room and finding him unconscious on the floor. He described the wait for the ambulance while the nurses had pumped at his dad's chest, and the wait at the hospital until the consultant came out and told him his dad was awake and Lucas could see him. He couldn't quite bring himself to describe the tiny part of him that had wished his father hadn't made it through. He described the time he'd been to Morning Rise in August when his father had been sober but still threw his dinner plate across the room at his son's head. 'I moved out of here to have him with me, but I couldn't do it.'

Charlie shook her head. 'It sounds like he needs professional care.'

Lucas nodded. 'I know.'

Trish frowned. 'So you're living on your own?'

'Yeah.'

'And do you like it?'

Lucas shook his head. In truth he hated it.

'So move back in here.'

'Really?'

'Please. We've had four housemates since you moved out and they were all nutters.'

Charlie nodded. 'One of them used to take a spatula in with them when they went to the toilet.'

'What? What for?'

'We don't know.'

Trish dropped her gaze to the floor. 'We don't want to know.'

'Okay.'

And then he was being hugged from both sides.

'You're not pissed off with me?'

'What for?'

'Well, lying, moving out. All of that.'

Both women laughed. 'Don't be ridiculous. You're part of the family Fake Alan. You don't get rid of us that easily.'

12

Christmas Eve, 2015

Jessica

Simon pulled an armful of DVDs from one of the boxes. 'Oh my god. You own some cheesy films.'

In reality Simon, and his lovely new boyfriend, Zac, weren't really helping. They were mainly mocking Jess's possessions. Zac pulled a couple of DVDs out of Simon's hands. 'You've got Christmas movies. We should watch one.'

Jess pursed her lips. 'We're supposed to be unpacking.'

Simon wrinkled his nose and looked around at the mass of boxes and piled up possessions that currently formed Jess's new lounge. 'Are you sure you don't want to keep it like this?'

Jess nodded.

The couple exchanged a look. Zac grinned. 'But we're all going to his tomorrow, so we could totally leave this 'til after Christmas.'

Jess folded her arms. Her 'assistants' had already set up the TV and DVD player and filled her fridge with 'new home' gifts of champagne and chocolates. Her bed was set up and made. She'd found the kettle and unpacked most of her clothes and toiletries. 'It's half past ten in the morning.'

Simon leaned towards her. 'On Christmas Eve. Normal rules don't apply.'

He was right. It was Christmas Eve. And it was gearing up to be a refreshingly relaxed and chilled out Christmas. Just her and Simon and Zac. Her mum and dad were in Leeds with her eldest brother's family. She didn't have Patrick to keep happy. The thought made her pause. That's what she'd done, wasn't it? She'd spent her marriage making Patrick happy and trying to keep him that way. This Christmas was going to be about her, and she was spending it with people who seemed to genuinely like her. 'All right. I'll get something to drink. You shove the worst of the mess out of the way and pick a film.'

Zac clapped his hands. 'Open the New House champagne.'

Jess stared at him. 'Still half past ten in the morning.'

He stared back. 'Still Christmas Eve.'

Jess knew when she was beaten. 'All right then.'

Simon followed her into her new kitchen. 'Thanks Jess.'

'What for?'

He shrugged. 'Being so nice to Zac. Mum was a bit . . . ' His voice tailed off. Jess didn't need him to explain how Mum had been. Their parents had never expressed any problem with Simon being gay, but had quickly developed the same aspirations for his perfect partner as they had for Jess's. They were waiting for a responsible, hard-working, and preferably, high-flying man to come along for Jess's brother. Zac was more of a free spirit. 'He's a lot younger than me.'

Jess handed the champagne bottle to her brother to open, while she pulled glasses out of the cupboard they'd only been unpacked into an hour earlier. Maybe a year ago stuff like Zac's age would have bothered her. She'd had a lot of time to think about what made relationships work since then. 'But he patently adores you.' She grinned. 'And quite right too.'

Simon leaned back against the worktop. 'I didn't expect . . . '

'What?'

'Another chance. After Anthony.'

'I'm happy for you. You deserve to be happy.'

She let Simon lead the way back into the living room, where Zac had spread what looked like her full stock of Christmas movies out on the floor. 'So what do you fancy? I'm thinking either *Miracle at the North Pole* or *Miracle on 34th Street*. You can't beat a small child experiencing a Santa-related life-changing moment at Christmas.'

Jess picked up the two copies of *Miracle on 34th Street*. 'Original or remake?'

Zac sucked the air through his teeth. 'Tricky. Normally I'd say original is always best, but Dickie Attenborough as Santa? What's not to like?'

Simon leaned through the gap between them and picked the *Miracle at the North Pole* DVD up from the floor. He shot Jess a look. 'I think we should watch this one.'

Simon was the only person Jess had told the whole Lucas story to. Even with Michelle she'd omitted the small detail of him being an international child movie star. It was Lucas's secret to tell, not hers. Jess pursed her lips. She couldn't really object without explaining her reasons and Zac, though lovely, probably wasn't the most discreet person in the world. She took a gulp of her champagne and let the bubbles fizz and tickle on her tongue. 'Fine.'

They shoved the remaining boxes to

one side of the room and squashed together on the sofa. The film hit all the right emotional Christmas marks. It was sweet but not sickly, and tugged at the heartstrings in the best possible way. The final scene saw Lucas's character back home in his suburban cul-de-sac after his adventure at the North Pole. Santa's sleigh stood in the road alongside him, and the big guy in the red suit crouched down to the young Lucas's height. 'So what would you like for Christmas now son?' he asked.

On screen Lucas furrowed his brow. 'Something for my mum. Something she lost when Dad went.'

Father Christmas frowned. 'You know I can't bring him back.'

Lucas nodded. 'I know but she lost something else. She lost hope. I'd like her to get that back.'

And, with a nod, Santa smiled the twinkliest of smiles, ruffled Lucas's hair, let out a hearty 'Ho! Ho! Ho!' and steered his sleigh out into the night.

It was ridiculously sentimental, but

that didn't stop the tears streaming down Jess's face. Hope. The fifteen year old girl who'd met Lucas in that kitchen had been full of it. Where had she disappeared to, Jess wondered. That girl had been happy to dive in with both feet. She hadn't been sensible when that perfect boy had tried to kiss her. She hadn't come up with problems or objections. She'd been brave enough to enjoy the moment. She'd been brave enough to hope.

Simon squeezed her arm. 'Love that film. Have you got the sequel?'

Jess shook her head. Even for her, that would have been a step too far. 'The sequel's awful.'

Zac jumped in. 'It's not really. It's exactly the same again.'

Jess nodded. 'Which makes no sense, because it's the same again, but this time Santa lives in Lapland instead of at the North Pole. You can't just move Santa.'

Simon laughed. 'So we'll agree that the sequel is an anathema but that this one is a classic.'

'Total classic.'

'It's twenty years old you know.' Zac turned the DVD box over in his hand. 'They're doing a re-release with a big premiere thing tonight in Leicester Square.'

Jess nodded. She'd read about it on the entertainment pages, telling herself she was interested in the nostalgic movie from when she was a kid, and that she wasn't desperate for news of Lucas. Of course there wasn't any. All any of the articles said was that Lucas Woods had disappeared from the public eye.

Simon glanced at the clock. 'We should get going. I've got seven types of veg to prep this afternoon.'

Zac rolled his eyes. 'There's only three of us. It's basically just Sunday dinner.'

Simon gave him a look. 'It is not Sunday dinner. It's a Christmas feast. And you're not doing anything until all my potatoes are peeled.'

Zac mouthed a weary 'So not going to happen' at Jess.

'Are you sure you don't want to stay over at mine tonight?'

She refused her brother's invitation. 'No. I'm going to unpack a few more things, and I think I've got something else I need to do.'

'On Christmas Eve?' Simon frowned.

'Yes.' She led the way into the hall and picked up her handbag and winter coat. It was a silly idea, a silly romantic idea, but watching the movie had made her think. And if she wasn't going to do it now, then when?

Christmas Eve, 2015

Lucas

Lucas lay on the bed in what was, apparently, his room again. He'd drunk too much to drive home the day before, and given that he was planning to move back in anyway, staying had seemed like a sensible option.

'Fake Alan!' The voice was accompanied by a knock on the door and, a second later, Cora shuffling into his room.

'I'm assuming they've told you that's not my name.'

She frowned and sat down on the bed. 'Well, we always knew that wasn't really your name, but yes. I wasn't even all the way through the door before Charlie cracked. I can't start calling you something different now though. It's too weird.'

'Fair enough. What are you doing here?'

'Just dropping off some food for tomorrow. I'm still coming for Christmas lunch.'

'Quite right too.'

She nodded. 'So what are you going to do now?'

And that was the question Lucas couldn't answer. He wondered if he'd been hiding because he didn't want to face up to his past, but caring for his dad, keeping in touch with the two girls

210

who'd been hurt in the accident, living with the constant guilt, all made it feel like dealing with the past was all he ever did. It wasn't the past that Lucas had trouble facing up to.

Cora cleared her throat. 'Or think about it another way. What do you really want?'

'In what way?'

'Any way you like. Work or life or relationships or family. What's the one thing? The thing that you want more than anything?'

'I guess I want to be happy.'

She shook her head. 'Well everyone wants that. Be specific. What do you hope for?'

Lucas had the beginning of the tiniest edge of the hint of a thought, but he couldn't put the words together.

'What's made you happy in the past?'

His face broke into a smile. The idea wasn't a beginning anymore. It was fully formed and screaming at him. He knew exactly what he wanted. He'd known all year. Lucas was a fool. He hadn't just known all year. He'd known since he was sixteen years old.

'I have to go.'

'What?' Cora jumped slightly as he leapt up from the bed.

'I have to go.' Lucas was suddenly buzzing. Time, so much of which had passed him by unnoticed, was suddenly precious. If something was to be done, then it was going to be done right now. 'She was right.'

'Who was right? Right about what?'

'About everything. Christmas is romantic.' He checked his watch. 'I have to go.'

13

Christmas Eve, 2015

It was three hundred and sixty four days since the last time she'd knocked on this door. What an incredible difference a year made. Last time she'd been numb; this time she was fizzing inside. She'd lost her temper with Patrick and it had felt liberating, and now she couldn't let go of the idea that it might not be too late. Years of disappointment had taken away her hope, and replaced it with a constant nagging fear. That wasn't okay. It was time to start hoping again. The door opened. Cora. Jess had to admit that she hadn't quite considered that. Cora folded her arms. 'Are you going to be doing this every year?'

Jess shook her head. 'I was looking for Lucas.'

One exquisitely sculpted eyebrow rose on the face in front of her. 'Lucas?'

'Alan. Lucas. Alan.' Jess shook her head. 'You know who I mean.'

The perfect face cracked into a smile. 'You've just missed him.'

'Right.' Setbacks hadn't really fit into Jess's thinking. Her plan, roughly speaking, had gone: One: Seize the moment. Two: Well, one was really the end of the plan. She'd seized but the moment had slipped out of her grasp. 'Do you know where he's gone?'

Cora shook her head. There was a silence. Cora unfolded her arms. 'You can come in and wait if you want.'

Jess didn't particularly want, but her only other idea was to pace up and down the street until he came back, and it was freezing outside. She followed Cora into the living room, which was full. Jess wasn't sure if that was better or worse.

Cora paused. 'So you remember

Liam? And this is Charlie and Trish.'

Jess nodded at the assembled household, but then something else caught her attention. The DVD. 'You know about this?'

'Yeah.' Cora sounded wary. 'Officially only since last night though.'

Jess stared at the poster. 'And you talked to him about it?'

Cora nodded.

Jess smiled, and let the feeling of hope rise through her belly again. 'I have to go. I think I know where he is.'

Across town Lucas pressed his finger to the buzzer and waited. No answer. That wasn't the plan. He wasn't fully sure what the plan was, but it definitely involved her being home. In frustration he pressed the buzzer and then the one above and below it. The intercom came to life. 'Jess?'

'Who is this?'

'I'm looking for Jess. Jessica. Flat four.'

The voice crackled. 'Not here any more. She moved out.'

'Do you know where she went?'

'Sorry mate.'

The intercom hummed for a second and then fell silent. So that was that. She wasn't here any more. He'd taken half a lifetime to work out what he wanted and now it was gone. He stuffed his hands in his pockets and turned to walk away. Inside his pocket his fingers wrapped instinctively around his phone. Lucas really was an idiot sometimes. He might not know where she was but, of course, he knew how to find out.

* * *

Jess stood on the edge of the crowd and tried to get her bearings. The cinema was at the far side of Leicester Square, and there was a fenced off area for the red carpet. The barrier was already lined with film fans, many of whom were dressed as elves or in the distinctive NHS glasses Lucas's character had worn at the start of the movie. Jess had to get to the front. That was the only way he'd see her. She wasn't normally the sort to push to the front. She was the sort to hang back and wait and see what everyone else wanted to do. And this is where it had got her. Alone on Christmas Eve getting bustled out of the way by people who thought their lives were more important than hers. Well no more. For once Jess was going to be the star. She stuck her elbows out to the sides and started to work her way through the mass of bodies. As she got to the front and rested her hand on the railing her phone vibrated against her leg. She squirmed to pull it out of her pocket and realised that she'd already hit answer as she was trying to get the handset clear of her jeans.

'Hello? Hello? Jess?'

'Hello.'

'Where are you?'

'Who is this?' She could hear herself shouting over the noise of the people talking on either side of her.

'I tried to find you.'

She pulled the phone away from her ear for a second and glanced at the screen. *Lucas*. Jess gasped. 'I'm here.

I'm waiting for you.'

'Where?'

'Leicester Square.'

'What are you doing there?'

'The movie thing. I'm waiting for you to come down the red carpet.'

There was a long pause on the other end of the phone. 'Leicester Square?'

'Yeah.'

'Wait there. I'll find you.'

* ★ ★

Lucas hung up the phone and started running. The tube would be heaving but it was still the quickest way. He wound his way through the packed bodies and squashed into a corner. It was going to take a while. What if she didn't wait? What if she had second thoughts? What if the whole idea of the girl in the kitchen was a mirage, a fantasy he'd made up at the worst time of his life? He remembered last Christmas; the taste, the feel, the realness of her. That hadn't been a fantasy. That had been something genuine and he'd stuffed it up. He checked his watch and willed the stops to fly by faster.

* * *

Jess watched the stars of the movie make their way down the red carpet, interspersed with a whole load of pop singers and TV personalities, many accompanied by perfectly dressed children who'd clearly been prised away from the nanny for half an hour to make a pretty picture for the paparazzi who had assembled opposite. An announcer was keeping the crowd entertained, drawing their attention to whoever was stopping to sign autographs, and grabbing people for thirty second interviews as they passed.

Jess let the hubbub wash over her. Lucas wasn't among the stars on the red carpet, but on the phone he'd said he was coming. Her head span slightly. He'd said he was coming, but the last few celebrities were making their way past and he wasn't here. She'd thought hope would be better than fear. Maybe she'd been wrong. If you dared to hope, you were daring to lose that hope all over again. She turned away from the barrier. Lucas had lied. He wasn't coming. She pushed her way forward.

The crowd parted before her.

Lucas.

She walked towards him, letting the bodies close back together behind her until they were inches apart.

He bent his head to her ear, and half-shouted over the crowd. 'What are you doing here?'

'I was looking for you.'

'Why did you think I'd be here?'

'Cora said you'd gone out, and I saw the DVD and they said you'd told them everything and I thought . . . '

He pulled his face back slightly and she could see the confusion on his face.

'I thought you'd sort of come to terms with your past or something.' It sounded lame as soon as she said it, but Lucas was nodding.

'I did. I think I have, but all this . . . '

He waved an arm at the crowd and the cinema and the red carpet. 'This *is* the past.' He was having to yell so she could hear, but the noise around them made it a completely private conversation. 'I went to find you.'

Jess shook her head. 'No! I came to find you, but you were out . . . '

'Looking for you.'

'Looking for me.' Everything was falling into place. He'd been looking for her. She'd been looking for him. Jess reached forward and wrapped her fingers around his. He bent his head towards her. Jess stepped back. Concern filled his eyes. Kissing him would be easy. Kissing him would be so right, but there were things she needed to say first, because she knew that once the kissing started there wasn't going to be much talking at all. 'I need to say sorry.'

'What for?'

'Last year. I overreacted.'

Lucas shook his head. 'I should have told you who I was.'

Jess swallowed. 'I should have given

you a chance to explain . . . ' She paused. There was something else. 'It wouldn't have made a difference.'

He nodded. 'It's okay. I can understand you not wanting to rush into anything after . . . '

'It wasn't that.' She felt him inch away from her. She squeezed his hand a fraction tighter. It was so hard to explain. She'd been cautious about romance her whole adult life. She'd believed the rules she'd heard. She'd believed that rebound things were a bad idea, and that you should take your time. She thought she'd learnt how relationships worked, but she'd learnt nothing that prepared her for how Lucas made her feel. 'It wasn't you though. I think I told myself it wasn't the right time. You gave me an excuse not to get close and I grabbed it.'

She could see the beginning of a smile in his eyes. 'Like maybe fifteen years ago wasn't the right time for me?'

'Your dad?'

He nodded.

'And now?'

He was quiet for a long long time. Jess waited.

* * *

Lucas thought about everything that had happened. He'd been a kid. He'd been a normal kid who'd made a completely exceptional film. It had changed his life, and the lives of the people closest to him. And then his dad had got off his face and driven a car into a group of pedestrians and everything had changed again. And somewhere amongst all that he'd met a girl, and even though he'd only known her for one evening, everything about her had been right. And then he'd met her again. And she was still right. And he'd thought that he was ready, but the past was always there, and now she had a past as well, playing on her mind and changing how she reacted to the here and now. The past wasn't going away, but maybe they didn't have to live there all the time. Eventually he spoke. 'Now is good.'

She smiled.

'What about for you?'

'I think I've learnt that now is all we have.'

She was right. Lucas was used to dealing with his past and worrying about the future, but right now was what mattered. He bent his head towards her again and this time she let his lips brush hers. Then she pulled away.

'What's wrong?'

'Nothing. But they keep announcing how child star Lucas Woods vanished from public view, and going on about how it's a great mystery, and you're standing right here.'

Lucas looked around at the crowd, all turned towards the bright lights and the shiny, famous people who'd been laid on for their entertainment. 'So?'

'So I don't mind if you want to go and . . . ' She waved a hand towards the red carpet. 'Be Lucas Woods for a bit.'

Lucas couldn't stop himself laughing. That seemed to be what everyone expected him to want. 'No. I didn't quit acting because of my dad's accident. I think I only kept going for as long as I did because he wanted me to. I grabbed an excuse as well.'

'One more question.' He knew what she had to ask.

'Why did you lie to me back when we first met?'

'I didn't.'

She narrowed her eyes.

'Well I did. I lied about my name, but that was all. I didn't want to be Lucas Woods any more. I wanted to be normal. I wanted to have mates, and meet a girl I liked and for it just to be simple. I wanted to do a job where I got to help people and nobody gawped at me. Alan wasn't a lie. Alan is more me than Lucas Woods, the movie star, ever was.'

She smiled. 'That's a good answer.'

He shook his head. 'It's a stupid answer, but I promise you, it's the truth.'

She glanced back towards the red carpet. 'So you're walking away from all this? No regrets?'

He shook his head. 'I'm not walking

away from that. I'm walking towards the thing I really want.'

'Which is?'

'You.'

★   ★   ★

Jess let the thought sink in. She'd worked so hard to make Patrick happy, but in the end what he wanted wasn't her. She'd given up on romance and miracles. She stopped believing that she could have perfection, but, in the end, there was no point giving up on miracles, because the miracles didn't care if you believed or not. They didn't reward effort, or beauty. Miracles were miracles. Love was love and all you could do was hope, and when your miracle came to find you, you could grab on and never ever let go.

She smiled and raised her lips towards his to claim her perfect moment, with her perfectly imperfect man.

We do hope that you have enjoyed reading this large print book.

Did you know that all of our titles are available for purchase?

We publish a wide range of high quality large print books including:
Romances, Mysteries, Classics
General Fiction
Non Fiction and Westerns

Special interest titles available in large print are:
The Little Oxford Dictionary
Music Book, Song Book
Hymn Book, Service Book

Also available from us courtesy of Oxford University Press:
Young Readers' Dictionary
(large print edition)
Young Readers' Thesaurus
(large print edition)

For further information or a free brochure, please contact us at:
Ulverscroft Large Print Books Ltd.,
The Green, Bradgate Road, Anstey,
Leicester, LE7 7FU, England.
Tel: (00 44) **0116 236 4325**
Fax: (00 44) **0116 234 0205**

THE BRIDESMAID'S ROYAL BODYGUARD

Liz Fielding

After being sacked from her job with a gossip magazine, Ally Parker is given a fresh start when her childhood friend Hope asks her to work PR for her marriage to Prince Jonas of San Michele. When Count Fredrik Jensson, head of security for the royal family, arrives, he makes it clear that Ally's past employment makes her unfit for her role. The fact that there's a sizzle between them from the moment they meet only makes everything worse . . .

ALWAYS THE BRIDESMAID

Jo Bartlett

Finally moving home after five years in Australia waiting in vain for faithless Josh, Olivia is welcomed back into the heart of her best friend's family on the Kent coast. Cakes, donkeys, weddings and a fulfilling summer job — all is wonderful, except for her unsettling attraction to Seth, who is moving to the United States after the summer. Is it worth taking a chance on love, or would it just lead to more heartbreak?

PAWS FOR LOVE

Sarah Purdue

Sam rescues animals and trains assistance dogs — but has less understanding of people! Meanwhile, Henry is desperate to help his young son Toby, who hasn't spoken since his mother died. Toby's therapist has suggested that an assistance dog might help the boy. Unfortunately, Henry Wakefield is terrified of dogs! But when Sam brings Juno into their lives, Toby begins to blossom and Henry starts to relax. Will Juno prove to be a large and hairy Cupid for Sam and Henry?